A Cry in the ...

The child she gave up for adoption eight years ago is missing, and Ava Simpson is convinced his life is in danger. Only one person can help her find the boy: Blake Tranowski, the birth father of the child. If only she can forge the courage to tell him of the existence of their son. . .

The anger Blake felt toward Ava when she dumped him nine years ago can't touch the fury he experiences when she makes her shattering revelation. Even more shattering is Blake's discovery that the boy really has gone missing. Why hasn't the adoptive father contacted the police? How is the man involved with a Mexican drug cartel? Is their son even alive? As Blake and Ava race against the clock to find their son, others are intent on stopping them. Even if it means killing them.

Some of the praise for Cheryl Bolen's writing:

Protecting Britannia **(Texas Heroines in Peril series)**
"It's fun to watch the case unfold in this nonstop action adventure...Graham and Britannia's second chance at love adds dimension to the story." – 4 STARS *RT Book Reviews*

Murder at Veranda House **(Texas Heroines in Peril series)**
"Murder at Veranda House has it all--sizzling romance, an intriguing tale of who done it, a fun cast of oddball characters, and a historic home that becomes a major player in the suspense." – *In Print*

With His Lady's Assistance **(Regent Mysteries, Book 1)**
Finalist for International Digital Award for Best Historical Novel of 2011.

"A delightful Regency romance with a clever and personable heroine matched with a humble, but intelligent hero. The mystery is nicely done, the romance is enchanting and the secondary characters are enjoyable." – *RT Book Reviews*

The Bride Wore Blue **(Brides of Bath, Book 1)**
"Cheryl Bolen returns to the Regency England she knows so well. . .If you love a steamy Regency with a fast pace, be sure to pick up *The Bride Wore Blue*." – *Happily Ever After*

With His Ring **(Brides of Bath, Book 2)**
"Cheryl Bolen does it again! There is laughter, and the interaction of the characters pulls you right into the book. I look forward to the next in this series." – *RT Book Reviews*

The Bride's Secret **(Brides of Bath, Book 3)**
(originally titled A Fallen Woman)
"What we all want from a love story...Don't miss it!"
– *In Print*

Novellas:

Lady Sophia's Rescue

Christmas Brides (3 Regency Novellas)

American Historical Romance

A Summer to Remember (3 American Historical Romances)

World War II Romance

It Had to be You

Inspirational Regency Romance

Marriage of Inconvenience

.

A Cry
In The Night
(Texas Heroines In Peril)

Cheryl Bolen

Harper & Appleton

Prologue

"Mom-meeee—"

It was the fragile yet curiously husky voice of child. A child of about eight.

This was not the first night his shrieks had torn through her like shrapnel, not the first time desperation had gripped his thin voice.

But tonight she was determined to save him. Save him from what? She did not know. All she knew was that he needed her.

"Mom-meeee—" His voice grew more distant. A steel door slammed. The already dimly lit corridor blackened. Yet she kept racing down the narrow hallway toward his voice. She threw open the cold, metal door. More blackness.

He screamed out again.

"I'm coming," she answered, her legs powering her through the next inky hallway.

Another steel door. More darkness. The boy's voice more distant. But she kept racing after him. This time she had to succeed.

Not like those other nights.

She was running so hard she could hardly breathe. Her legs felt heavy, as if she were trying to run through taffy. *I can't stop*, she told herself. *He needs me.*

One after another, she opened more steel doors and ran through endless black corridors, but the child's voice — without losing even a fraction of its urgency — kept growing more distant.

Then she woke up.

Her heartbeat still thundered. Perspiration drenched her nightgown. It took her a moment to realize where she was, to realize she had once more been revisited by the same recurring nightmare.

Chapter 1

Blake Tranowski was the last man on earth Ava Simpson would have come to for help. At eighteen, she had burned every last bridge that linked her to him.

But desperation and urgency had brought her to him today.

For Blake Tranowski was the only man Ava Simpson could turn to for help.

The last she had heard of him was seven years ago. His promising baseball career destroyed by a knee injury, he had exchanged a baseball uniform for a policeman's uniform in Dallas or San Antonio. One call to her Aunt Jolene gave Ava the right city. "I reckon he's the closest thing to a celebrity Dry Creek, Texas, ever had," Jolene had told her. "They say he's rich as an oilman now." Aunt Jolene pronounced *oil* as *oh-el*.

"Being a policeman?" Ava asked, brows plunging with astonishment.

"On, no! He now owns a high fallutin' private eye agency in San Antone."

Exactly what Ava needed.

Blake was her last hope. For the past six

days she had frittered away a year's worth of sick leave. And she was not one step closer to finding the boy.

The boy whose name she did not know. The boy whose terrifying wails seared into her sleep night after night like a bullet tearing through flesh.

She had no more time to waste. The boy needed her. She knew that as surely as she knew the name of the man who had fathered the child.

A little more digging provided Ava with the name of Blake's agency. Lone Star Investigations was located in a modern mid-rise office building on San Antonio's Loop 410. Even from the freeway she could read the firm's name in the same distinctive navy and red lettering the agency used on its website.

As she parked her car on the surface lot near the feeder road, she stayed relatively calm. She stayed calm even as she strode through the building's brass and glass revolving entry door. Not until the elevator deposited her on the fifth floor — where Blake's agency was located — did her heartbeat begin to roar.

When she spoke to Lone Star's pretty blond receptionist, Ava's voice trembled. "I need to talk with Mr. Tranowski."

"Do you have an appointment?"

"No." Ava shook her head. "Just tell him

Ava Simpson needs to speak to him on a matter of some urgency."

The blonde smiled stiffly. "Are you a client?"

"Just an old friend," Ava said with a firm shake of her head.

"If you'll just take a seat, Mrs. Simpson."

"It's Miss," Ava corrected as she moved across the reception room's sleek slate floors and slid into a deco-style leather chair.

By its very restraint, the office was opulent—opulent being an excess of understated quality.

Only then did she become aware of the sultry jazz music, so clear and sharp that a combo could have been playing not ten feet away. She searched for its source, and after a moment detected speakers built into the ceiling of the same color.

The state-of-the-art office was a far cry from the sagging ranch house where Blake and his four brothers had grown up. If the investigation business was doing this well, he was probably driving a luxury import instead of his old Chevy pickup.

A moment later, the receptionists' stiletto heels tapped against the floors as she came to stand before Ava. "I'll show you to Mr. Tranowski's office."

The strike of the woman's shoes against the broad hallway's slate terminated at a corner office. Both women stopped abruptly, but as the door eased open, the receptionist retreated.

Which left Ava facing Blake alone.

Her heartbeat stampeded. At first all she saw were his smoldering black eyes. His somber gaze poured over her, but she could no more read the expression on his darkly handsome face than she could erase the nine years since their estrangement. She took in his coffee-colored brown hair, his athletic body, the starchy blue jeans and cowboy boots he wore. How could the past nine years have changed him so little — yet so much?

A flood of sweetly torturing memories swamped her. Her former affection for him had *not* embellished his rugged good looks. Not one particle. He was even more good looking than she remembered. Definitely more muscular. His face now emanated a solemn maturity that would have been alien to the cocky all-state pitcher he'd been a decade earlier.

"It's been a long time, Ava," he finally said, swinging the door open wider.

She stepped into his office, then gazed up at him again. "I was afraid you might not want to see me."

He laughed bitterly as he shut the door. "If I gave a damn. . ." His smile revealed teeth as white as Xerox paper. "But I don't."

Even though she deserved his contempt, it still hurt. She strolled into the office that was drenched with dazzling sunlight and sank into a chair in front of his desk.

"I didn't expect you to be jumping up and down with glee to see me. Our parting wasn't particularly amicable."

"We don't need to go into that." He leaned back in his chair. Like all the chairs throughout the office, it was upholstered in soft lamb's skin dyed the same blue as the company's logo. "What's this urgent matter that brings you here today? I'm assuming your visit's professional."

She nodded. "You're obviously a very successful investigator, and I need your help."

"With what?"

She shifted her weight. She balled her hands into fists. She drew a breath. God, this wasn't going to be easy. "I need you to locate someone."

"Piece of cake." Rolling his chair closer to the desk, he sat up straight and poised fingers to the keyboard. "Name?"

"I don't know."

His eyes flashed with anger. "Why don't you just start from the beginning?"

It was not a question.

"It's an adoption case," she said. "Only adult adoptees have the right to open records. I need to locate the whereabouts of a juvenile adoptee."

"Why the urgency?"

"The child's in danger."

His brows lowered. "And you know this because?"

"I . . . I can't explain. But I'm certain the child's in danger."

"Come on, Ava." He threw his arms up. "I'll need more than that."

"You don't believe me?"

"I've never known you to lie."

"I'm positive the child is in danger."

"What kind of danger?" He pronounced the words as if he were talking to a kindergartener.

She sagged against the back of her chair. "I don't know."

"Then how in the hell do you know the kid's being jeopardized?" He rolled his eyes. "One. More. Time. Start at the beginning."

"You'll think I'm crazy."

"Look, I've known you your whole life, and I'll vouch for your level-headedness."

"Thank you. I *have* always been level headed. I've never had dreams like this before. Well, except once. Sorta. And it turned out to be real."

He nodded. "I remember. Something about that frickin scholarship of yours."

Her senior year of high school she had dreamed that the application for her Texas Leaders of Tomorrow Scholarship had been lost in the mail. After she woke up, she called the university in Austin. They had not received her application, and that was the final day to apply. Her father had driven a hundred and thirty miles to Austin to hand deliver it. "That dream was worth more than a hundred thousand dollars."

Their eyes locked again. Neither would break the gaze. Neither would speak. Finally, she sighed. "That's why I'm so sure the child's in grave danger. I keep having this recurrent dream where he cries out for me." Her voice cracked. "I have to find him." Last night was the twelfth straight night she'd had the same nightmare.

"Tell me about the kid." He could not have sounded more disinterested had he been discussing the weather.

"That's what I need you for."

"I'll need the birth state, city, child's date of birth, and name of the birth mother. Can you give me any of that?"

Her heartbeat tripped. "Yes," she managed in a feeble whisper. "All of it."

He wheeled his chair closer to the see-through desk and settled his fingers over the keyboard. "State?"

"Texas."

He typed. "City?"

"Austin."

His fingers skipped over the keys. "Date of birth?"

"He turned eight last week. May tenth."

Blake nodded, his brows squeezing into a v. Then he typed in the date. "Birth mother?"

"Ava Simpson," she whispered.

He froze.

She knew he was doing the math.

His angry gaze whipped to her, his dark eyes glittering with rage. "The kid's mine!" He had never sounded more furious. Not even that last day.

"Yes, he is."

"And you didn't see fit to tell me?" His tone and the hardened look on his chiseled face reverberated with contempt.

"It was for the best."

Both his hands thwacked the desk. "The best for who?" His voice was so loud she half expected an intercom query from one of his employees.

"All of us. You. Me. The baby. If you'd found out about the baby, you'd have let go of your dream of playing professional baseball. A minor league player who was only twenty years old could not support a family. I know you, Blake. You would have thrown aside your dreams to do what you thought was right. And I had dreams, too. I was just graduating from high school and didn't want to let go of my dream of being a cancer researcher. I thought I was doing what was best for the baby. I thought he'd go to a home where he'd be showered with love and all the material possessions a child could want."

Her stomach clinched. She would never have given him up had she an inkling that he would ever be endangered.

"What *you* wanted, what *you* thought was for the best. Your audacity's disgusting. Did it never occur to you I had the right to know I'd fathered a child?"

Tears filled her eyes. "I'm sorry."

"You sure as hell are!" Anger shook his voice. With unsteady hands, he pushed out of his chair and stormed to the floor-to-ceiling windows which afforded a view of downtown San Antonio.

Swiping away tears with the back of her hand, she stared at his back, at the crisp white shirt stretched across his broad shoulders. He had used the word *audacity* to describe her actions nine years ago. He had been correct. What right had she to exclude him from such a monumental decision? How could she have been so arrogant at age eighteen to think she had enough experience at life to make wise decisions?

For the next five minutes he stood there, his back to her, his blistering anger filling the room like toxic gases. Were it not for her fears for her child's safety, she would never have exposed herself to such wrath, would never have sought so painful an interview with the only guy she had ever loved.

Finally he turned to face her, his contempt as blatant as a slap in the face. "I have the right to know everything."

"I understand that now."

"You were pregnant when you dumped me, weren't you?"

She blinked back tears. "That's why I broke it off. If you'd known I was having your baby, you would have insisted we marry. Marriage would have robbed both of us of our dreams."

"So you didn't even tell me," he said with disgust. His black eyes bore into hers. "Did you tell anyone?"

"Only Daddy. He helped me hook up with Catholic Services. After I impressed upon him that I had no intention of marrying you." Until her ninth month, her father had never stopped singing Blake's praises, never stopped encouraging her to marry Blake.

"So you went to Catholic Services in Austin?"

Her face solemn, she nodded. "They took care of the medical services and the adoption."

"You. . . saw the boy?" he asked, his husky voice cracking.

A sob broke from her throat. "The sec-c-c-cond he w-w-was born. Then they whisked him away. His hair was dark." She sniffed. "Like yours."

Blake closed his eyes as if in pain.

A moment later he asked, "You don't know anything else about him?"

"Nothing. That's why I came to you."

"And you don't really know if he's in

danger. You just dreamed that he is." Mockery tinged his voice.

"Right. Except I do know." In a hoarse whisper, she added, "Though I hope to God I'm wrong."

"I do, too." He moved toward her. He came so close she could smell his spicy aftershave. As his face drew nearer, she thought he was going to kiss her. Then blazing fury flashed in his eyes, and he growled: "I'll get you the kid's address, then I never want to see you again."

* * *

After Ava left, he asked Tiffany to hold his calls. He had a hell of a lot to digest. It felt as if a sharp line drive had splintered his chest. Nothing had ever stunned him more than the revelation that he had a son. A kid old enough to play Little League baseball, and Blake hadn't even known of his existence. Bitter rage surged through him.

The betrayal Ava had dealt him nine years ago couldn't touch what she'd hurled at him today. How could he ever have felt such tenderness for her?

As clearly as he recollected his most recent case, his thoughts flashed back to those first two years he had spent in the minors. He'd been so damned homesick. And so totally in love with Ava that he'd never even looked at another girl. Hell, he had begged her to marry him as soon as she finished high school.

The very memory of such powerful feelings

— feelings stronger than anything he'd experienced in all the years since — smothered him anew with pain so intense, it was physical.

He would have chucked everything to have been able to make her his wife. Not money, not baseball, not any prospective career could have meant more to him than she did.

But all she ever talked about was her dream of being a cancer researcher, of finding a cure for the disease that had killed her mother.

What really sucked was that he still wanted her. When he had first taken in her slim, blond loveliness today, desire bolted through him. Thank God he'd been able to turn on the bravado. Thank God he had learned to turn his back on his undeniable attraction to her.

His knowledge of her had come at a great cost. A cost that kept climbing higher.

It tore him up to know he had a son, a boy being raised by another man. Dammit. Losing the boy hurt even more at this place in his life than it would have nine years ago. With his thirtieth birthday only a month away, Blake's thoughts had increasingly been turning to family.

He wanted one. He wanted kids. He wanted a marriage as solid as his parents'. He wanted a real home, not that icy penthouse he resided in. His riches only underscored how much he needed to have a family to spend them on.

Problem was, ever since Ava had burned him he had never trusted another female. Four years he had given her. All for nothing.

Enough thinking about Ava. He stalked to his desk. He needed to find his son. Not that the kid could possibly be in any danger. His chest constricted.

Could he?

Chapter 2

He had neither wanted to nor intended to get involved in Ava's case. All he had wanted was to get the kid's name and address and hand it over to her. He didn't want to see the boy, to know anything about him. He needed to forget the kid was his. The boy already had a father.

But Blake had not counted on two unexpected reactions, the first being the awakening of his own protective instincts. What if the kid *was* in trouble? He would never be able to forgive himself if he did not make sure the boy was OK.

Not that he gave any credence to Ava's silly dreams.

His own perverse curiosity about the boy was also unexpected. As painful as it would be, he *did* want to get a glimpse of the kid.

Getting his hands on the birth records had not been too difficult. Especially with help from an old friend who was the best there was at hacking into government systems.

Seeing his name listed in black and white as the birth father had left Blake shaken —

shaken and exhilarated at the same time. It was like seeing the opposing team come from behind to beat you in the ninth. After you'd pitched a no-hitter.

Somehow, his name emblazoned on the official adoption document made the case even more personal, made his determination more immediate.

And it left a hell of a lump in his throat.

His chest had tightened when he saw that his son had been given another man's surname: Meecham. The boy was Mick Meecham. He smiled at the name Mick. Mickey Mantle — the Mick — had been his dad's favorite player of all time. It was fitting that his son bore that name.

Fitting as well as depressing.

Blake spent a couple of hours after Ava left trying to find out everything he could about Mick's family. He was pleased to learn they still resided in Austin.

That afternoon he made the ninety-minute drive to the state capital. Judging from their lakeside address, the Meechams were well off. Very well off. Posing as an old family friend of Walter Meecham, Mick's father, Blake queried neighbors in the affluent neighborhood and learned what school Mick attended.

Getting into the boy's class would be more difficult. But he had worked that out.

He drove his pickup to the west Austin elementary school and, with leather portfolio in hand, strode to the office, introducing himself to the secretary as Dr. Michael Jabbic. "I've been retained by the Meecham family to observe their son Mick in a classroom environment."

He handed over a professionally printed card that identified him as a child psychologist. She need not know the real Dr. Jabbic had been one of Blake's clients.

A woman sitting at a desk farther away from the front counter addressed him. "You've picked a bad day. Mick Meecham's not here today. In fact, he was out of school all week last week."

Blake felt as if he had been kicked in the gut.

"She's the attendance clerk," the secretary explained.

Gathering his composure, Blake tsked. "Darn! I told his parents a couple of weeks back I'd try to get here right away." He shook his head. "Been swamped."

"I tried to call his house this morning," the attendance clerk continued. "It's not like Mick to miss a day. He had perfect attendance in kindergarten, first, and second grades."

Oh shit!

A young, bespectacled man came strolling from an adjacent office and offered Blake a hand. "I'm Mr. Milstead, the principal of Walt Disney Elementary. I'm surprised the Meechams would seek a psychologist to observe Mick. He's a great kid."

Blake tried to exude a calm he was far from feeling. "I believe they wanted to know how he interacted with other children, being an only child and all."

"Sometimes an only child of much-older parents does have problems, but Mick's very well adjusted," Mr. Milstead said.

"I'm sure his parents will be glad to know that." Blake turned back to the attendance clerk. "You weren't able to get a hold of Mr. or Mrs. Meecham?"

She frowned, shaking her head. "No."

Not what Blake wanted to hear. "Say, would it be possible for me to ask a few questions of a couple of boys in Mick's class?"

The principal's brows rose, then he nodded. "If you don't keep them out of class more than five minutes." He turned to the secretary. "Ask Alex Ramirez and Christopher Holzman to come to the office."

While they waited for the boys, Mr. Milstead said, "Mick's had a remarkable year. He won the Punt, Pass & Kick competition for the third grade, and he also won the Big Shootout basketball free-throwing competition."

Blake wished he hadn't been told.

When the boys arrived, the principal introduced them and offered his office.

"I have a couple of questions to ask about your classmate, Mick Meecham," Blake said, once they were alone. "By the way, do you know if he's sick?"

Alex shrugged. "He missed Saturday's baseball game." The boy frowned. "We lost."

Dammit, the boy — his son — played baseball, too!

"Which league do you guys play in?" Blake asked.

"Windham Park."

"Was Mick at practice last week?"

The boy shook his head.

"I went to Mick's house two or three times, but he's not there, either," Christopher added.

That gut-kick feeling walloped Blake again. He tried to mask his worry. "I guess the family decided to take a trip."

"I guess so," Christopher said. "You could check with Mr. Meecham's work. He owns the Angus Steak Houses."

"Thanks, I will," Blake said, forcing a smile as he got to his feet.

Back in his truck, he whipped out his cell phone and called his office. "Hey, Tif, I need you to call the corporate offices for the Angus Steak House chain in Austin. I've got to know if the CEO, Walter Meecham, is in Austin right now. Do whatever it takes to speak to him personally. ASAP."

* * *

Maybe she shouldn't have taken off work. Maybe she should have gone back to Houston. Hanging around the hotel, doing nothing, was getting to her.

She left the balcony overlooking the lake and returned to her hotel room, snapping on the television in the hopes of catching the five o'clock news and weather.

Even though Austin was less than two hundred miles from Houston, completely different news stories dominated the broadcasts. In Houston, the big story had been the tragic death of three firefighters. For days the media had delved into violations of fire codes that, if addressed, could have prevented the deaths.

In Austin, every newscast focused on the high profile trial of Mexican-American drug lord Carlos Pacheco.

"After five weeks of dramatic testimony, the murder trial of alleged drug kingpin Carlos Pacheco is expected to go to the jury early next week," the attractive female reporter said into her microphone. "The state's star witness is projected to take the stand Thursday - - "

A knock sounded at Ava's hotel room door. She wondered who it could be. No one knew she was here, and it wasn't as if she had requested extra towels or anything.

"Who is it?" she asked, her heart thumping as she neared the door.

"Blake."

A thousand scenarios rushed to her mind. He'd said he never wanted to see her again.

Could the visit be prompted because he'd learned something terrible? Or perhaps he had not learned anything at all. What if he'd discovered that the child was living far away in a place like Alaska?

And why hadn't she changed out of the Longhorn tee shirt that made her look like a shapeless pencil?

She unbolted the locking devices and opened the door. "How did you - - "

"It's my job. Finding people."

He was good. And, oh boy, was he good looking, all hulking shoulders and long, muscled legs. He wore another starchy white shirt with the blue jeans and boots that must be a staple in his wardrobe. "Have you found him?" No beating around the bushes for her.

"Yes." He frowned as he stepped into the room. "No."

"What do you mean?"

"Let's discuss it over dinner. I haven't eaten all day."

She was secretly pleased he had reneged on his intentions of never seeing her again. "Just give me a sec to change tops."

* * *

The beer garden favored by university students and state legislators alike was located a few blocks from her hotel. Since it was still May, it wasn't too hot to sit outside.

They sat on a wooden picnic table beneath the verdant limb of a spreading oak and ordered beers and burgers.

"He's in Austin, isn't he?" she asked as soon as the waitress left their table.

"Yes — at least, that's where he's lived his entire life."

"But he's M.I.A."

Blake grimaced. "I think so."

"Tell me everything," she said solemnly.

"His name's Mick Meecham."

A smile softened her face. "Like Mick Jagger."

"I was thinking Mickey Mantle."

They both laughed. A mirthless laugh.

"His adoptive father is Walter Meecham, who owns the Angus Steak Restaurants around Austin."

"There are one or two in Houston now, too. We're talking serious money."

He nodded. "I think the money originally came from Mrs. Meecham. And, yes, they're seriously rich. They have a huge mansion overlooking Town Lake."

"Any siblings?"

"Nope. He's an only child. His adoptive parents are the age of our parents." He took a copy of a newspaper clipping from his pocket and showed it to her. "This is a picture of the Meechams at a charity gala."

Ava stared at the photo. Not at the man. At the woman whom her son would address as his mother. The slender woman was likely in her late fifties, with whitish blond hair slicked back into an elegant knot at the nape of her neck. Her strapless dress not only showed off her deep tan but also provided the perfect backdrop for her dazzling diamond choker.

A bolt of pure jealousy strummed through Ava. It hurt to think of another woman raising her little boy.

Even if it was her own decision.

"Are the . . ." She could not bring herself to call them her child's parents. "Are they in Austin?"

He shrugged. "I'm pretty sure the mother and Mick are not. I'm trying to find out about Meecham."

"Do you have a photo of . . . the boy?"

"No." He sounded as disappointed as she felt.

"You found out what school Mick attends?" She liked his name, liked the fact that she could now attach a name to him.

Blake nodded. "He hasn't been there all week. The attendance clerk hasn't gotten an answer by calling their home phone, either."

Blake's confirmation that the boy was missing caused her stomach to roil. "Oh, God," she whispered hoarsely. "Do you think there's a possibility I might be right about him being in danger?"

"No, I don't. The kid's going to be fine. I'll show you."

That the child had not been in school all

week confirmed her fears. They sipped their beer in silence. She wasn't fooled by Blake's machoness. The fact that he was with her — whom he had vowed not to see again — was testament to his worry.

"How did you explain yourself? At the school?" she asked a few minutes later.

He flipped her Dr. Jabbic's card. Before he could return it to his pocket, his cell phone rang. "Tranowski," he answered. He listened for a moment, nodding, then he caught Ava's attention. "Write this number down."

She snatched a pen from her purse and wrote the number on a napkin as he called it out.

"Good job, Tif," he said before terminating the call.

He gazed at Ava. "Meecham's in town. I'm going to go see him."

"Today?"

He looked at his watch. "It's just after five." Rising from the bench, he added, "I'm going to try to see him now." He secured two twenties beneath his frosty mug and started to walk away, Ava on his trail. "Sorry about the dinner," he called over his shoulder. "I'll drop you off at the hotel."

"I want to go with you."

"Sorry, babe. I work solo."

Once they got into the pickup she said, "Why don't you just tell Mr. Meecham the truth? That you're the birth father and want to make sure the boy's all right?"

"No can do. I'd be jeopardizing a friend who hacked into the birth records for me."

"Then how are you going to explain yourself to Mr. Meecham? I don't think your Dr. Jabbic persona will work for this."

He bit at his lip. "But a doctor might."

"Yes, a doctor could — or some kind of medical professional." A second later, she said, "I've got it!"

He inched out of the parallel parking spot while watching his rear-view mirror. "What?"

"Let me go see Meecham. I've got my identification from the University of Texas Health Science Center."

His eyes narrowed. "Are we on the same page?"

"I thought I could be assisting the national Center for Disease Control - - - "

"Because a child at Mick's school has contracted a highly contagious disease?"

God, this was scary. She and Blake could still finish each other's sentences. Just like they had done a decade earlier. "Exactly."

* * *

Blake drove her to the corporate offices of the Angus Steak House chain located on Oltorff Road. Before she got out of his truck, she clipped on the photo ID she was required to wear at work.

Inside, the older woman who manned the reception desk refused Ava's request to speak with Mr. Meecham. "Mr. Meecham's not in. Can someone else help you?"

"Only Mr. Meecham. I know he's here," Ava bluffed. "I need to talk to him about his son. It's very important."

Her lips pursed, the receptionist swallowed, then in an icy voice said, "I'll need your name."

"Ava Simpson."

The receptionist wrote it down, then punched some buttons on the phone. "I'm sorry to disturb you, Mr. Meecham, but there's a woman here from ..." She tossed a glance at Ava's name badge. "From the University of Texas Health Science Center who says she needs to speak to you about your son, that it's important."

After she hung up, she told Ava to take the elevator to the second floor, which would open onto Mr. Meecham's offices.

Exiting the elevator, Ava immediately recognized Walter Meecham from the photo in the newspaper as he strolled toward her, his stooped shoulders indicating a man even older than the mid-sixties she judged him to be.

She extended her hand. "Mr. Meecham?"

"Yes," he said gruffly, his hand — like the rest of him — stiff when it clasped hers. "You've got news about my boy?"

It hurt her to hear him — not Blake — claim their child. "Yes, Mr. Meecham. Can we speak in private?"

He nodded, his brows lowering as he led him into his inner office.

With its richly paneled walls, plush red carpet, and gilt of picture frames and shiny brass lantern scones, his office had the feel of an English gentleman's study. He closed the door and stood facing her, his expression somber. A flicker of emotion passed over his face. Could it be fear, she wondered. "About Mick. . ." he began.

"A child in Mick's class has contracted a serious and highly contagious disease. I'm assisting the Center for Disease Control in evaluating and inoculating children who might have come in contact with the infected child."

"When did the child get sick?"

Obviously, Walter Meecham was hoping the exposure had occurred after Mick's absence. "Week before last," she answered. "The disease wasn't isolated until today."

"You say the kid's actually in Mick's class?"

She nodded.

"I'll see that my son is inoculated."

"It's not in your hands, Mr. Meecham. This is a matter of public health. I need to see Mick."

"Tell me what symptoms to look for."

"We need to do blood testing. I have instructions to locate him and take a blood sample." She gave him a stern look. "Where can I find your son?"

"He and his mother are out of state. I'll see to it that he gets the proper tests."

"I'm afraid that won't be good enough. Only those authorized by the Center can give your son a clean bill of health. If you'll just give me the location. . ."

"I can't do that. They're . . .in transit."

"And I can't leave here until I have the location of your son."

"You sure as hell can. If you don't get off my premises, I'll call the police."

Her heartbeat pulsed. "Good! Because I've got the law on my side. Your son could be a potential menace to the public health. Perhaps the police can ensure that you comply."

"I cannot comply with your request. Not today." He looked at his Rolex. "Get back in touch with me in the morning."

Her gaze flicked to a mahogany credenza where a framed photo drew her attention. She strolled to it and lifted a five by seven of a boy in a baseball uniform. The smiling, adorable little guy had Blake's dark eyes and hair, Blake's square jaw. He even had Blake's smile.

An incredible sadness drenched her as she realized the magnitude of her loss. Of Blake's loss. "Is this . . ." She could not bring herself to call this replica of Blake, Meecham's son."Mick?"

"Yes."

A compulsion to possess this photo gripped her. "I'll need your secretary to make a copy of this photo for our records."

He punched his intercom. "Helen, the young lady's bringing you Mick's picture. Copy it for her before she goes."

* * *

Once Meecham was sure the pushy woman was gone, he picked up his phone and called down to the receptionist. "Do you have the name of the woman from the medical center, the woman who just came to my office?"

"Yes, Mr. Meecham. It's Ava Simpson. I checked it with her identification badge."

"Good." He hung up and quickly punched in another number. "What do you know, Estrada, about a woman who came snooping around my office, asking questions about my wife and son?"

"What in the hell are you talking about?"

"You don't know anything about her?"

"Hell, no! What did you tell her?"

"Nothing. I said they were out of the state."

"You got her name?"

"Ava Simpson. She said some kid in Mick's class has a contagious disease, and she needs to check out all the kids who came into contact with him. Her badge is from the University of Texas Health Science Center, which I *thought* was located in Houston."

"We'll check it out." Estrada slammed down the phone.

* * *

"You can't deny that the man's hiding something," Ava said to Blake over dinner — at the same beer garden — an hour later.

He shrugged. "Just because he's hiding something doesn't mean the boy's in danger. Be rational, Ava."

"You didn't see him. The man was cold. He gave me the creeps. Don't you think a parent's normal reaction at being told his child may have contracted a deadly disease would be horror?"

"I don't know what it feels like to be a parent," he said, bitterness in his voice. "You saw to that."

She drew a deep breath. Tears sprang to her eyes. "I saw his photo."

"Mick's?"

"Yes."

Blake's dark eyes held hers. She knew exactly what kind of emotions were stirring within him. She understood that longing to get a glimpse of their child. She understood the desire for the unobtainable, the feeling of deep, unquenchable loss.

"I couldn't help myself," she said.

"You didn't steal it?"

She shook her head. "I had it copied."

He swallowed, still glaring at her. "I don't

know if I can stand to see it."

What she had to say next was going to be difficult, maybe even more difficult than telling him he had a son. "He looks just as you must have looked at his age."

The haunted look that swept over his face broke what was left of her heart.

"Let me see," he finally said.

As she went to fetch it from her purse, it occurred to her that this single piece of paper was her most precious possession. She would have it professionally copied and cherish it until her dying day.

Blake took it and stared at it for a long time. And when his eyes watered, the rent to her heart cracked a little deeper. A moment later he handed it back and attempted to speak casually. "Good looking kid."

By then, her tears gushed. She couldn't speak. All she could do was nod.

There had been a time when the sight of her crying would have distressed Blake. But that time was as distant as the memory of sultry summer nights at the baseball field in Dry Creek, Texas.

Now he was as unmovable as a chunk of stone.

Several minutes later, her emotions pushed beneath the surface, she returned to their previous discussion. "Mr. Meecham didn't even ask if the other little boy was alive or dead. I tell you, it's unnatural!"

"You're expecting him to display the emotions of a female. Men don't wear their hearts on their sleeves."

She swallowed. There was a time when Blake wasn't so macho, a time when he *did* wear his heart on his sleeve. She wished she hadn't destroyed that man.

While she had no right to expect him to display any tenderness toward her, she knew he did care about his son. Their son. His don't-give-a-damn air could not conceal the emotions Mick's photo had elicited in the man who had given him life.

And the very fact that finding the boy had take precedence over all his other cases proved that finding their child was extremely important to Blake. "I know you're worried about him, too."

His face grave, he nodded. "Yes, I am concerned."

"So what do we do now?"

"I won't leave Austin until we find Mick."

Chapter 3

She woke earlier than usual the following morning, shimmering sunlight arrowing into her hotel room from the gap in the draperies. Normally, she would have been mad at herself for not securing them better. But normally she would have felt robbed of sleep. Surprisingly, she felt well rested this morning, more rested than she had felt in weeks. When she realized why she was so well rested, she sprang up, her heartbeat racing.

She had not dreamed of Mick. For the first night in almost two weeks, she had not been tortured by the recurring dream.

Could that possibly mean the one thing she dreaded most? She felt perverse to even think such disturbing thoughts, but she kept thinking *Mick is dead.*

Her first instinct was to call Blake, but she decided not to. He gave no credence to her dreams

She felt a blinding compulsion toward this child she'd never even met. Perhaps it was because she had no one else. Her father was her only immediate family still living, but he had a happy family apart from her now that he had remarried, retired from his job, and traveled around the country in an RV.

Because she led so lonely an existence, no one would really care if something happened to her. Least of all, she. If there was the remotest chance she could help Mick, she would gladly put her own life on the line.

She flung back the bed covers and stumbled to the coffee maker. Who cared if caffeine was unhealthy? She was going to have a cup of coffee. Or two. Walter Meecham couldn't be expected in his office until nine. Nearly three hours away.

She flipped on the TV news. From the courthouse steps, a pretty reporter said, "The state's eye witness to the brutal execution-style murder of Orlando Garza is expected to take the stand later this week in the Carlos Pacheco murder trial. The state alleges that Garza was Pacheco's rival over the lucrative south Texas drug trafficking turf."

What Ava really wanted was the weather. She grabbed the remote and changed stations. "Today's high is expected to hover in record territory," the weatherman said. "Temperatures could top ninety six." Sheesh! And it was only May.

Too bad she couldn't wear shorts to Mr. Meecham's office.

* * *

Nine o'clock sharp she strolled into the corporate offices of the Angus Steak House chain. This time she walked past the reception desk and took the elevator to the second floor.

Making eye contact with the bespectacled secretary, Ava said, "Tell Mr. Meecham that Ava Simpson has returned."

"He's expecting you?"

"Yes."

The woman punched the intercom. "Miss Simpson's here to see you, Mr. Meecham."

There was a pause, then he said, "Have her come in."

As Ava entered the well-appointed office, Meecham's glare made her feel uncomfortable.

"Who do you really work for?" he demanded.

Her stomach lurched. "I am employed by the University of Texas Health Science Center."

"And you're *not* working for the Center for Disease Control."

Her shoulders sagged. "No, I'm not."

"And there's no sick child in Mick's class, is there?"

"No," she said in a barely audible whisper.

A look of rage swept over his craggy face. "Are you a police woman?"

Why would he think her a police woman? "Of course not!"

"Then why in the hell did you come here telling me a pack of lies? What business is it of yours to go snooping into my family's affairs?"

"Your family's affairs appear mighty suspicious."

"That's none of your concern."

Their eyes locked. If he knew she was a phony, why wasn't he calling the police? The man obviously had something to hide. Intense pain seared through her. Not a pain that could be eradicated with any kind of physical treatment or drug. She hoped to God nothing had happened to Mick. "Where are you wife and son?"

"One of my wife's out-of-state relatives became ill. She had to go to her, and she didn't want to leave Mick."

Ava refused to disconnect her gaze from his. "So, where are they? Which state?"

He hesitated for a millisecond. "New York."

"I'd like a phone number."

"Over my dead body. This is none of your business." He rose, glaring at her. "Get the hell out of my office."

"I think, Mr. Meecham, you're hiding something, and I plan to get to the bottom of this. I'm going to the police." She turned to leave.

"Wait!"

She turned back, her gaze frosty.

"Who in the hell are you?" he asked.

"I'm. . ." She swallowed. "Mick's birth mother."

His eyes widened as his gaze poured over her like a bucket of ice water. "I see no resemblance."

"That's because — judging from the photo on your desk — he looks like his father."

His jaw tightened. "What day was Mick born?"

"May tenth."

"That would be easy enough for you to discover. Can you tell me the name of the hospital where he was born?"

"Breckenridge."

He took a deep breath. "Maybe you are his birth mother. Maybe not. Let's assume you have his best interest at heart. I will set up a face-to-face meeting with you and my son next week if you can just give them time to return to Austin. I only ask that you not disclose your true identity to him."

She did not know if she was strong enough to actually be close enough to hug the boy and not be able to. She shook her head. "I don't need to talk to him. I only want to see him, to know that he's OK."

"I beg you to give me a week."

She bit her lip. "I'll think about it." Then she turned and left, pummeled by an onslaught of powerful emotions.

By the time she reached her Honda she did not know what to do. She really wanted to go to the police, but first she needed to talk to Blake. She owed him that.

* * *

Blake had decided the night before to take a room at her hotel. She hoped he was still there.

As her car snaked through the hotel parking garage, she was pleased to see Blake's white pickup still in the same spot where he'd parked it after dinner the previous night. She slid her car into the space next to it, from the corner of her eye watching Blake move toward his truck.

Just as she went to open her car door, Blake shouted at her. "Get down!"

In a blinding flash, she followed his gaze and got a glimpse of a black SUV slowing behind her car. At the same instant her window shattered.

That's when she complied with Blake's demand.

She saw the blood before she felt the searing pain in her shoulder.

Then horrifying, explosive sounds surrounded her. Gunshots.

From the crack in her partially open door, she was powerless not to watch as Blake drew his weapon and dropped to his knees, moving toward her as he fired at the SUV. More glass shattered.

She was terrified Blake would be killed.

Another volley of gunfire followed, then

tires screeched as the car behind hers peeled out of the garage.

"Ava! Are you all right?" Blake moved to her and threw open the car door.

"Are you?" A sob tore from her throat.

"My God, you've been hit!"

She frantically shook her head. "I'm OK. You could have been killed."

He yanked his cell phone from his jeans pocket and called 9-1-1. "I've got a gunshot victim in the parking garage of the Town Lake Plaza Hotel. We need an ambulance quick." After terminating the call, he stripped off his shirt, folded it into a tightly packed square, then pressed it against the site of her wound, just above her armpit. "Hold still," he said, his voice gentle.

"I must have been followed."

"From where?"

"I went to see Walter Meecham again this morning."

His eyes turned to chips of ice. "Without telling me?"

"You would have tried to talk me out of it."

"And with good reason. You obviously put yourself in danger."

"See, I told you the man was evil!"

"Maybe I should have listened."

She was shocked the ambulance arrived so quickly. Less than five minutes later, the paramedics were taking her vitals and loading her onto a stretcher.

"I'm coming with her," Blake told them.

"Sir, you'll have to follow in your own vehicle."

"Where are you taking her?"

"Breckenridge."

She would be really glad when they gave her an opiate. The pain was getting worse by the minute. Her only compensation was the look of concern than transformed Blake's face as he solemnly watched her being loaded into the ambulance. "See you in a couple of minutes," he promised just before the rear doors slammed shut.

* * *

Blake did not know who to be maddest at: Ava for rushing off to confront a possibly deranged man without even telling him. Or the slime balls who tried to kill her — and him. Or himself. He had done a piss poor job of handling this whole case.

Throughout the five-minute drive to the hospital, he was still shaken from the shootout that could easily have claimed his life. He couldn't shake the feeling of pure terror that had slammed into him when he saw the shooter level his gun at Ava. He couldn't purge from his mind visions of blood soaking her blouse. And he was still dazed that he'd actually shot at another human being. Though he'd had to draw his weapon several times when he was a patrolman, he'd never actually had to fire at anyone.

It was a hell of a lot different than target practice.

At the hospital, he assisted her with the admissions paperwork, unconsciously clasping her trembling hand in his, unconsciously speaking to her in a soothing voice.

He was relieved that she saw a doctor almost immediately. The dark-skinned young doctor hurried into the room and introduced himself as Dr. Patel. "I understand you took a bullet?"

Ava nodded, bowing her head in the direction of her bloodied shoulder.

The doctor began to probe at the wound, then asked her to move her shoulders, which she did somewhat reluctantly. The youthful doctor nodded approvingly, then asked her to move her arms, and lastly her fingers. "You're a lucky lady," the doctor said in his sing-song accent. "No broken bones. No damage to nerves or major blood vessels."

"Does that mean I won't need surgery?"

"Yes. In fact, we don't even stitch these closed. You need to wash the site a couple of times a day with mild soap. No strong antibacterial. Then you need to cover with sterile dressing."

"I don't have to stay in the hospital?"

"No. Just let me clean the wound and send you on your way with meds."

Blake moved back as a nurse stepped

closer to the gurney to assist the doctor while he cleaned the wound. Blake might be a big guy, but he was a real wuss when it came to witnessing medical procedures. Heck, even the smell of a hospital caused his stomach to go queasy.

He was amazed he hadn't passed out back in the parking garage when he saw such massive amounts of blood soaking Ava's clothes, amazed that he'd been able to stench the flow of her bleeding.

"Blake? Do you need to put your head between your legs?" Ava asked.

So she remembered his propensity to queasiness in hospital settings.

"I'm not going to pass out. How are you doing?"

She winced. "I've been better."

"Hey, the doc says you're one lucky little lady." She *was* little. Her wispy size had been one of the traits that had attracted him. All those years ago.

"Let me tell you, lady," Dr. Patel said, "if that bullet had hit you a couple of inches lower, you would not be here. And I do not mean here at Breckenridge Hospital."

Relief flooded Blake.

Once the doctor had taped gauze over the wound, he asked her if she could take Vicodin, and when she answered in the affirmative he wrote out a prescription.

He started to hand it to Blake, but Ava

said, "I'd like to see it. I'm a registered nurse."

"Oh really? Where?" The doctor asked.

"Actually I'm a cancer researcher at the tumor institute in Houston."

Dr. Patel's interest perked. "You finding a cure?"

She smiled. "Not a cure, but we're having great success with a new chemotherapy that kills only the cancer cells without destroying healthy tissue." She looked at the prescription. "No antibiotics?"

"No. I'm not expecting infection. It's not like you were rolling around in the dirt. But if there's any redness, any increase in pain — and especially if there's fever — you are to return to the hospital immediately." The doctor went to leave the room, then turned back. "No alcoholic beverages with that Vicodin."

When the door opened, a fortyish man in a sports coat and slacks came strolling into the room, offering his hand to Blake. "Detective Grierson. I understand the lady here suffered a gunshot wound from an unknown assailant."

Blake and Ava both nodded.

Grierson moved to Ava. "I'll need to fill out a report, miss."

Her worried gaze flashed to Blake.

"I'm afraid she saw very little," Blake said. "The perps were in a vehicle that must have been following her. They were behind her, but

I got a glimpse of them."

"Whoa! Let's start at the beginning," Grierson said.

He asked for Ava's name and all her contact information. Then he asked, "Where did the shooting occur?"

"In the parking garage of the Town Lake Plaza Hotel."

He wrote down the information. "And you don't know the assailants?"

"No. And my friend's right," she said, meeting Blake's gaze. "I didn't see much of anything. I was concentrating on parking my vehicle, then I saw Blake - - -" She indicated Blake. "Walking toward me. Then he shouted. And I got shot."

The detective eyed Blake. "I'll need your name, sir." He proceeded to write down Blake's contact information.

Then he turned back to Ava. "So you didn't actually see the shooter?"

"I turned and got a blurry glimpse of a black SUV with two men in it. The one on the passenger side was holding a silver colored, very large revolver."

"TDL number PSL 937," Blake said.

The detective's brows rose. "Good work. Not many men could get a license number when someone's shooting."

"I didn't during the shooting. Got it as they drove off."

"Did they shoot at you, too?" the officer

asked.

Blake nodded. "And I returned fire."

"You have a permit to carry?"

Blake showed him his private investigator's identification.

"Did you hit either suspect?"

"Possibly. I heard a Spanish cuss word."

"No clue who they are?"

"None," Blake said.

The policeman looked at Ava.

She shook her head.

"Can you give me a description?" This time the detective directed his question at Blake.

"Two young Hispanic men."

"How young?"

"Not as old as me. I'm twenty-nine."

"Did both men have guns?"

"At first, it was just the guy riding shotgun, but when I fired back, the driver slammed on the brakes, then he got his hands on a weapon and started shooting."

"How would you describe the first shooter, the passenger?"

"His head was shaved. Medium build. Tats on his arms, but I couldn't read them. Letters, not pictures."

Grierson's pen raced over the page, then he looked up. "And the driver?"

Blake shook his head. "I'm no help there. My impression is he was a lot like the other guy. Fairly young. Shaved head. Tattoos. But I'd never be able to pick him out of a lineup."

"What about the make and model of the car?"

"A Hummer."

The detective nodded, then turned to Ava. "You're sure you don't know who these guys are?"

"I've never seen them before."

"Is there someone who wants you dead?"

Her gaze flicked to Blake's.

He almost imperceptibly shook his head.

"I can't think why anyone would want me dead."

Grierson's attention returned to Blake. "Is Miss Simpson a client of yours?"

"No. Just an old friend."

The detective's gaze swung back to Ava. "Pretty big coincidence that you've got a PI guarding you when you're definitely in jeopardy. In fact, I find it hard to believe you didn't hire Mr. Tranowski to protect you against those thugs." He paused, his eyes narrowing. "Why don't you come clean with me?"

"Hold on," Blake said, his voice firm. "Don't talk to my friend like that. Just fill out your damned report and find the bastards. Secondly, I do not provide protection services. I'm an investigator."

Ava offered the policeman an apologetic smile. "I *am* telling you the truth. I never saw those men before, and I don't know why anyone would want me dead."

"Obviously," Blake said, "It's a case of mistaken identity."

The detective's glance flicked to Ava. "If there *is* someone threatening you, you would do best to let the Austin PD protect you."

"Nobody's threatening her. Rest assured if that were the case, I'd insist Ava report it to the police."

The detective frowned and gave Blake his card before he left.

Alone together in the room, Blake approached the bed and gave her good arm a gentle squeeze. "We're not going back to that hotel."

"We should have told the policeman about Walter Meecham."

"I don't want to hide anything from the police, but we can't very tell them about your crazy dream without having them think us a pair of crazies."

"I know. But I also know Walter Meecham has to be behind that attack on me." She took a deep breath. "On us."

"Give me twenty-four hours. Then I'll dump it all on the Austin PD"

"What do you have in mind?"

"A couple of things." He withdrew his cell phone from his pocket and punched in his partner's cell phone number. "Pete," he began when his best friend answered, "this personal matter I've been investigating in Austin is a lot more serious than I'd first thought."

"Serious as in drawing weapons?"

"Yeah. I can't fill you in on everything right now, but I need some heavy surveillance. First, I need bugs at a residence located at 254 Town Lake Circle. The homeowner should be gone all day today. Don't know if there's any domestic staff there to contend with. Also, I want the house put under surveillance twenty-four/seven, and I need to be in direct communication with the field operatives."

"On your cell?"

"Yes. Also, I need the homeowner's business watched."

"Name?"

"Walter Meecham, CEO of Angus restaurants. Corporate address, 20071 Oltorff. And Pete, I need one more thing."

"What?"

"I need an I.D. for Texas plates number PSL 937."

"No problem. Where are you now?"

"Breckenridge Hospital."

"Are you all right?" Pete asked, his voice hitched with worry.

"I'm fine. An old . . . friend of mine took a bullet."

"Shit! This really is serious. Is. . .is your friend OK?"

"She'll be fine."

"Maybe I should come to Austin," Pete said.

"I'm a big boy."

"Answer me this. Were you shot at?"

Blake hesitated. "Yeah."

"I'm coming!"

"Please, Pete, hold off. Let's see what we can learn from the surveillance. Hopefully, we'll know more by tomorrow."

After he hung up, he had misgivings. He hated withholding information from Pete. And from the police. He should be working with the police to find the perps who tried to kill Ava and him, to lock up that damned Meecham. Ava must have been right about the guy.

The very thought that Meecham might have killed the boy made Blake feel as if he'd been hurled down a flight of stairs.

But for the time being, he'd be working solo. He couldn't very well tell the cops or even Pete that the whole thing started because Ava had dreams. They'd think he and Ava were candidates for that state mental institution on Lamar Boulevard. He needed a bit more evidence before he could disclose the nature of the investigation.

Meecham was obviously in touch with the thugs who tried to kill them. Now Blake needed to record just one incriminating conversation between Meecham and his henchmen.

Hopefully, by tonight he could go to the police.

He just hoped to God the boy hadn't been . . . He couldn't say it, even to himself. But logic told him he was too late to save the boy.

His gaze flicked to Ava. A knot lodged in his chest as he watched her small bosom rise and fall beneath the hospital gown. Even with remnants of blood streaking her silvery blond hair, she was still beautiful. Not the kind of beauty one saw in flashy movie stars who wore five-inch high heels. Ava's beauty was delicate and quiet. Just like her.

As he sat there drinking in her soft loveliness, he could not dispel the fear that had gripped him when he thought she had been killed. No matter what she had done to him, he could not bear the thought of a world without her.

Of course, he wasn't about to reconcile with her. Miss Career First probably wanted no part of him or any other man!

The disgusting thing was, he still wanted her.

The mellow sound of her voice, a glimpse of her very nice, softly rounded figure still aroused him as acutely as it had when he was a teenager. And when she turned her pretty little porcelain pale face to his, he had to fight himself not to smother those pouty lips with kisses.

"Who's Pete?"

"My partner, Pete Alvarez."

"You two started the agency together?"

He nodded. "We were on the San Antonio PD together. Pete was a detective, and I was just a lowly cop who knew a lot about computer investigations."

"You always were a wiz with computers. I suppose that's a pretty necessary skill for running a high-tech detective agency."

He shrugged. "You gonna leave the hospital in that gown?"

"You want me to wear the bloody blouse that was cut off of me?"

"No. I'd better go buy you something."

"Unless you want to get my suitcase from the hotel."

His lips folded into a grim line. "Neither of us is going near that hotel. Those lowlifes are bound to expect you to return so they can finish the job."

"You may be right."

"So where do you want me to get the clothes?"

"I honestly don't care. Just get me shorts and a top." She eyed his undershirt. "And get yourself a new shirt."

He looked down at his chest and laughed. "What size do you wear?"

"One."

He cleared his throat. "What about. . ." His gaze dropped to the sweet swell of her breasts.

"A bra?"

He nodded.

Her cheeks flushed. "This is too embarrassing."

"It's not like I haven't seen them before. . ." Their eyes connected as if by some magnetic force. "Touched them," he murmured. God, the thought made him horny as hell.

She turned away. "Thirty two. B."

* * *

He was not terribly concerned that he would be followed. The dirt bags likely did not know who he was or what vehicle he would be driving. Still, he would be on alert, be cautious.

Since he hated to leave Ava alone for a minute, he raced to the closest store to the hospital, careful to make sure no one was following. Surveillance was one subject he knew a lot about, and he was sure no one was tailing him. At the department store, he grabbed the first shorts he saw. They were hot pink. He snatched a top that matched, then he rushed to the lingerie department and searched for the thirty two B's. A lacy cream-colored one seemed to stand out from the others. He grabbed it, then went to the men's department and selected another white shirt to replace his.

Thirty minutes after he left, he strolled back into her hospital room. Strangely, relief poured over him when he saw that she was still there. Unharmed. He vowed to himself not to let her out of his sight until this ordeal was over.

He tossed the bag on her bed, and she examined his purchases. "You did well."

"Need some help getting out of that hospital gown?" he asked.

"I . . ." Heat flared between them as their eyes met. "I'm not sure. There's nothing on under it."

"I know," he said, grinning wickedly.

Chapter 4

She went to playfully slap at him, but the action caused her to wince.

His worried gaze dropped to her wound, then he rushed to her, his voice gentling. "I'm sorry."

"It's OK. Just turn around, and I'll get myself out of this bloody gown."

He turned his back and tried to block the vision of her bare, ivory flesh. Easy as driving blindfolded.

She groaned, then sighed. "I guess I *am* going to need your help. I can't seem to put my arm behind me in order to get out of the sleeves."

"Here." He moved to lift one side of the gown off her good shoulder. "I won't gawk at your breasts."

"I know. You've seen them before. And they're nothing to write home about."

But they were worth writing home about. They were exquisite. Like priceless crown jewels.

They both laughed as he gently removed the gown. "You can put on the bra while I turn my back, then I'll fasten it for you."

More torture while he visualized those tantalizing pink nipples. While he hardened like a jutting rock.

It got even worse when his hands brushed against her back as he hooked the bra. His memories flashed back to those steamy nights in his first pickup, to the insatiable way they had never been able to get enough of each other. Her very touch had been to him like flame to dynamite.

And she had felt the same.

Except she'd been able to walk away from him, something he would never have been strong enough to do. He wasn't sure he could do it even now.

Especially knowing that her life was in danger.

Somehow he managed to help her dress without exploding.

She gazed up at him, her mossy green eyes as innocent as a child's. Not a trace of the lust that threatened to consume him. "Where to?" she asked sweetly.

He drew a fortifying breath. "I'm not sure. Hotels and motels are definitely out." The thought of taking her to a motel ignited a fresh wave of hunger. "Maybe we should go back to San Antone." Mindful of her injured shoulder, he lifted her off the table.

"No! I can't leave Austin. Not until I know . . . one way or another."

She did not have to say more. He knew what she meant.

And he could not have given voice to the fears, either. "Are classes over at the university?"

She gave him a puzzled look. "Yes. Finals ended yesterday."

"Then a lot of dorms and apartments have been vacated. Maybe we can make a deal with someone who's paid up until the end of the month."

"I know of some neighborhoods that are almost exclusively populated by students. I doubt if the city's changed that much since I graduated."

He offered his arm. "Let's go."

* * *

She decided not to remind him about getting the prescription filled. She'd rather suck it up and keep a clear head.

Besides, she knew how Vicodin affected her. She'd be jumping Blake's bones before she could get the cap back on the prescription bottle.

He'd always affected her in *that* way. She was so juiced up from his glances and touches back in the hospital room that she could barely concentrate on giving him the directions. Even the sight of his long fingers gripping the steering wheel brought to mind the ways he'd once pleasured her with those same fingers. Her mouth went dry. "Turn right on M.L.K," she instructed. "It's the next light."

A couple of minutes later they were cruising down a tree-lined street where small apartment units coexisted with 1930s bungalows.

"What about that guy?" She pointed to a college-age male stuffing bursting garbage sacks into his sporty SUV. "I think that's bedding he's got in those bags."

Blake swerved into the same driveway, threw the truck into park, and leaped from the vehicle.

Since he'd left the key in the ignition, she could still lower the windows in order to overhear their conversation.

"Moving out?" Blake asked.

The skinny blond kid slammed shut the rear door of his vehicle and eyed him suspiciously. "Yeah." His cautious glance darted to Ava.

"My girlfriend and I are looking for a place to sublet until June first. I'd like to strike a deal with you."

"What kind of deal?"

"Let me finish out this last week of your lease."

"It's my name on that lease. I'm the one responsible for any damages."

"You got a roommate?" Blake asked.

"He's already gone back to Dallas."

"Then I'd like to do business with you.

What's your monthly rent?"

"We each pay seven hundred."

"I'll give you a grand for the last couple of weeks of the month." Blake opened his wallet and began to count out hundred dollar bills.

The boy's eyes rounded.

"You can take down my license plate number and the info on my driver's license," Blake said. "It shouldn't be hard to come after me if there are any damages."

"Hey, man, it's a deal!"

"How soon before you can clear out?"

"Give me five minutes."

Ava smiled.

"OK if my girlfriend comes inside where it's air conditioned? She's not feeling well."

She liked being called Blake's girlfriend. And wished she didn't.

"No problem. But they're supposed to cut off the power tomorrow."

Blake groaned.

"I'll call the electric company," Ava said, climbing from the pickup. "What's the address here?"

"Four twenty seven Evergreen."

She took a pen and paper from her purse and wrote it down.

Minutes later she had the unpleasant task of telling Blake the power company couldn't get there until Thursday.

He glanced around the sparsely furnished house until his eye caught a window air conditioning unit. "Enjoy cool air while you can."

She walked from room to room. The bare hardwood floors throughout the tiny two-bedroom house looked as if they needed refinishing. She wondered how much beer had been spilled on them over the past few decades by partying college students. The double-sized beds in each of the bedrooms had been stripped of bedding, revealing slender, sagging mattresses that should have been replaced years ago. "Looks like we need to shop. We'll have to get linens."

"And food."

Their tour of the premises ended in the old-style kitchen, which was the only room without wood floors. The small, utilitarian stove and refrigerator stood on asphalt tiles that looked as if they needed a good cleaning. But she couldn't think about cleaning now. Not with the throbbing pain from her shoulder radiating down into her arm at each movement. "You go. I'm pooped."

"Sorry, babe. I'm not leaving you alone. Not until this mess is cleared."

"I couldn't possibly go anywhere until I wash my hair." She glared up at him. "In case you haven't noticed, my hair is streaked with blood."

"You can wear the baseball cap I keep in my truck. When we get back, I'll help you wash your hair."

The vision of him shampooing her at the kitchen sink caused her to smile.

* * *

By the time they returned to the house nearly two hours later, Ava could barely gather the strength to stand up, but she could not go another minute without washing her hair.

"You sit down while I put the stuff away," he said.

"How about you grab that shampoo and one of those new towels and help me wash this mess first? It can be drying while you put the stuff away and make dinner."

He set the bags on the counter, then began to remove his shoulder holster and the huge pistol it encased.

She edged away. "Oh, please, don't set it on the table! I'm terrified of those things."

He walked into the adjacent living room and carefully placed them on the coffee table.

Returning to the kitchen, he rummaged in the grocery sack until he found the shampoo. From another bag, he retrieved a fluffy white towel. "Is mademoiselle ready?"

She nodded and moved to the sink.

After he shampooed her hair and tightly wound the towel around her head, he steered her to the small, Formica-topped dinette table and pulled out one of its two chairs. "Feel bad?" he asked, setting a gentle hand at her waist as she moved to sit down.

"I feel like hamburger meat."

To her complete surprise, he swept her into his arms and strode into the living room, depositing her on the well-worn sofa. "I'm sorry you feel so crappy, sorry I couldn't allow you to rest."

"I'm glad you didn't leave me alone. I probably would have been terrified over my own shadow."

"With justification. You've been through a lot today. Now you need to relax and let me bring you something to drink." He straightened up and swatted his forehead. "Your prescription!"

She shook her head. "I don't need it. It will only put me to sleep, and I need to talk with you."

His face softened. "Are you sure? You've got to be hurting pretty bad."

"Just a little," she lied. "The ibuprofen in my purse ought to take the edge off the pain."

"Then let me get you a drink to take it with."

Why did he have to be so darn sweet? And so stupendously handsome? How in the heck was she going to be able to spend the night with him and not do something she hadn't even contemplated in nine years?

She had never wanted anyone but Blake. Then and now. She had mistaken her feelings for him as puppy love. Something she would get over. And while her memories of their love faded, no other man had ever made her feel the way Blake made her feel. No other man had ever appealed to her in the primal way Blake did.

She was only now coming to realize what she and Blake shared had not been puppy love. It was the real deal.

Was. He hated her now. Even if he was being really, really nice. Because of her injury.

He handed her a glass of cola. "OK if I get the ibuprofen out of your purse?"

"Sure. Thanks."

"I remember the time - - -"

"I got mad when you went fumbling in my purse?"

"Yeah. I was looking for - - -"

"The birth control pills you insisted I take?" Her lids lowered. "I didn't want you to know they made me sick. I couldn't take them. I was afraid you wouldn't have sex with me any more if you knew I wasn't on the pill." Having sex with him had been even more important to her than her compulsion to make straight A's.

She couldn't believe she was having this conversation with him. It was as if she had gotten doped up on pain relievers.

He came to sit beside her. "Is that the real reason why you wouldn't tell me about the baby? You thought I wouldn't want the kid?"

She couldn't remove her gaze from his

anthracite eyes, couldn't rid her thoughts of the intimate union she craved with this man. "I can't remember what I thought," she said breathlessly. "I knew you'd insist we get married if I got pregnant, and I didn't think either of us was ready for marriage or for kids." She began to cry.

His arms closed around her. Her face nestled into the comforting solidity of his chest. And she sobbed, inarticulately sputtering out the words: "Now I wish I had told you, wish we had gotten married."

And not just because of that precious little boy she'd given up.

He eased back and framed her tear-stained face with two rugged hands. The pads of his thumbs stroked her cheeks, his index finger brushed the plane of her nose as he spoke softly, like a night whisper. "The only reason I wanted you to take birth control pills was because I didn't want you forced to marry me. I wanted you to become my bride of your own free will."

"I see so clearly now. You were much wiser then than I gave you credit for. It was I who was the stupid one."

"Because you forced us to break up? Or because you gave up our child?"

Without a second's hesitation, she answered. "Both."

That one little word, uttered with such naked honesty, opened her to his rejection.

Seconds dragged before she could bear to meet his gaze. What if he gave a chortle of disgust?

Even when her lashes lifted, she could not read the smoldering look in his dark eyes.

Until he crushed her into him, devouring her mouth with a wet, searing kiss.

She shuddered when she felt his cool tongue slide into her mouth. Massive doses of Vicodin couldn't have made her any more receptive to this man. It was as if every place his magic hands touched turned to electrically charged pulse points. She could not steady her rapid breathing. She could not keep her swirling hands from pressing into his muscled back. She could not pull away from him if the room were in flames.

And she wasn't convinced it wasn't.

She wanted him so potently that she lost all sense of pride, lost any inhibitions she had cultivated during the last several years of casual — docile — dating of other men.

Nothing about Blake was docile. He was volatile. Inflammatory. And without a doubt the sexiest man she had ever known.

Together, they fell back, stretching out side by side.

He lowered the scooped neck of her tank top and pressed his mouth to her lace-covered nipples. The more he slickened, the sharper she felt them pointing, the wetter the circle in the center of her became.

His skillful hands found the soft flesh inside her thighs. She widened her legs, moaning softly as her hips raised slightly. If he didn't find her moist core soon, she would begin to beg shamelessly.

He began to toy with her. His fingers slipped inside her panties, grazing her seam, parting her, then receding.

God, but she wanted more!

She reached down and cupped his swollen arousal, stroking him until he groaned and raised himself over her. He snapped open the waistband of her shorts and shoved down her zipper as she lifted herself so he could remove first the shorts, then her panties.

His simmering gaze lazily stole over her. And he groaned again.

She began to move against the movement of his hand, rocking up and down until her entire body shuddered.

At that moment she knew what it was to lose control totally. Something she had not done in nine years.

* * *

Nine years seemed a lifetime ago. He was so different in so many ways then than he was now. And so was she. But one thing had not changed: her physical reaction to him. Way back when, he'd had to be the one to try to keep their relationship respectable. He'd never stopped trying to protect her, trying to keep from getting her pregnant, trying to conceal that the slender brainiac who was the smartest girl in the school turned into a brazen sex pot whenever they were alone together. He had always been the one who tried to avoid being alone because he knew what would invariably happen when others weren't around.

He and she were like two compounds that when joined together became something entirely different. Something explosive.

Her effect on him had not changed, either. He wished to God it had. He wished he didn't possess these strong feelings toward her, wished he didn't give a damn, wished like hell he could be strong enough to reject her.

She could still ensnare him like a hunter's trap.

Even after he had brought her to climax with his hands, she wasn't satisfied. "I want to feel you inside me," she murmured.

Which was exactly what he wanted.

She reached to unzip him. Then to caress his bulging arousal. He pushed her hand away, poised above her — careful not to touch her shoulder — and thoroughly made love to her.

The contentment that seeped into every cell in his body was something he had not experienced in nearly a decade.

His cell phone rang. He didn't give a damn. No way was he answering.

But what if Pete had learned something

about Mick?

Groaning, he sprang to his feet and snatched the phone from his discarded jeans.

Chapter 5

"Tranowski," he barked into the phone.

"Ever heard of Carlos Pacheco?" Pete asked.

"The drug lord?"

"One and the same."

"I read about his trial in this morning's *Statesman.*"

"The Hummer belongs to him."

Blake fell into the nearest chair. "How in the hell can their sleazy stuff be connected to a presumably reputable businessman like Meecham? Or to Ava?"

"Who's Ava?"

"The bullet catcher."

"Looks like you and this Ava have really gotten yourself in some deep doo doo."

Pete had no idea how deep. "Can you get me an address?" He wouldn't mind a drive-by to see if he could spot the shaved-headed slime balls.

"I'll work on it right now."

"Anything on the surveillance?"

"Just one very interesting thing."

"What?"

"Bugs were already all over the place."

Could the police already have Meecham under surveillance? Blake's brows dipped. "That is suspicious."

"Yeah, I thought so, too. Anyway, we've got the Oltorff location under surveillance, too, and we're working on infiltrating the building with a fake electrician."

"Good. Keep me posted."

"And you be careful. These guys are as low as they come."

Blake already knew that. But he did not know why in the hell they wanted Ava dead. Or how Meecham could be connected to them.

There had to be a connection. Even if Meecham did strike Ava as being evil, nothing in his demographic pointed to possible involvement with a Mexican drug ring.

As Blake disconnected the cell phone, Ava sat up, draping the pink striped tank top across her breasts. "What's going on?"

"The Hummer's registered to Carlos Pacheco."

"The guy from the trial?"

"Yep."

"You think the guys who shot me work for him?"

"There's a good chance of it." Trying not to gawk as she began to dress, he hurriedly dressed and went to the kitchen where he took the hairbrush from the still-full Walmart sack. "You need help with your hair?"

"Thanks," she said with a shake of her head. "Since my right arm — or should I say shoulder? — is still OK, I'll be able to manage." She began to run the brush through her hair, which was now dry. "Somehow this business has to be connected to Walter Meecham. I told you I didn't like him. No wonder he's rich! He's in cahoots with criminals."

"You have nothing to base that on."

"You didn't talk to the man. He gave me chills. He was as cold as an iceberg."

"That may be, but these Mexican drug cartels don't usually mingle with Anglos."

"As much as I don't like Walter Meecham, I do find it a stretch to picture a sixty-five-year-old successful businessman involved with murdering drug dealers."

"Especially since the man doesn't need money. His wife was loaded when he married her, and his restaurants are very successful."

"What if they're not so successful? What if he needs to bail them out?"

"If it's a publicly traded company, that information should be readily available." He got his laptop and booted it up. Less than ten minutes later, he shook his head. "Struck out here. Angus Steak Houses are not publicly traded, nor is any kind of Meecham company headquartered in Texas traded on the New York Stock Exchange."

"So if a company's having solvency problems, what do they do?"

"A company having solvency problems would have a tough time borrowing money."

"Then wouldn't they be likely to take on investors?"

His eyes narrowed. "Are you thinking what I'm thinking?"

"That Walter Meecham and Carlos Pacheco have entered into a business arrangement?"

"Tell me everything Meecham said to you this morning."

She set down the brush. "The minute I walked into his private office, he knew everything: knew I wasn't from the Center for Disease Control, knew there was no sick child in Mick's school, knew I was lying."

"Meecham couldn't possibly have the investigative resources to have learned that."

"But Pacheco's organization could."

"They sure as hell could. I wouldn't be surprised if they don't have at least one Austin cop on their payroll."

"So when I left his office yesterday, he asked Pacheco's goons to look into the situation?"

He nodded. "And he obviously had them there to follow you when you left this morning. To follow you and to silence you."

Her hand cupped her mouth. "That would explain why he so willingly let me leave."

"Let's back up. How did you identify

yourself?"

"As Mick's birth mother."

"And his reaction?"

"He asked questions about Mick's birth, and when I obviously provided the right answers, he said that if I would wait until next week, he'd let me meet Mick."

"Next week? You're sure he said next week?"

She nodded.

"That's puzzling. If he were trying to get rid of you — and I mean permanently — wouldn't it have been easier to brush you off by promising you could see Mick tomorrow?"

"That's true."

"Where did he say Mick is?"

"The liar said they were in New York, but I know he had to be lying because he hesitated a second before he answered my question about Mick's whereabouts."

"In this day of cell phones, his whole explanation is pretty bogus."

"He was so obviously lying."

"What else did he say?"

"Nothing really. I was in and out of his office in less than two minutes."

"There's too much that just doesn't add up. I know you don't like Meecham, but I cannot believe he'd harm Mick. The neighbor I talked to said Meecham was crazy about the kid. And the fact Mick's had perfect attendance every single year — until last week — points to the fact Mr. and Mrs. Meecham have their priorities in the right place."

"Perfect attendance? How'd you learn that?"

He shrugged. "At the school."

"Did you. . ." Her voice softened. "Did you learn anything else about him?"

"The principal said he's a great kid."

Tears began to puddle in her eyes. He had to turn away. All of this was too damned painful. "I also learned that Mick's apparently a good athlete."

A sob tore from her chest. "Just like his fa-fa-father. His real father." Her splintered voice had a childlike quality.

He moved to her and drew her up and against his sternum, his fingers threading through her shoulder-length hair.

"I'm . . . so afraid something's happened to him," she whimpered.

It could seem pretty incredulous for her to have such powerful feelings toward a child she'd never met. Except he had those same feelings. Protective instincts he had been unaware of had not only kicked in the last two days but they'd damn near overpowered him.

She buried her face into his chest. A moment later her shoulders began to shake with the wrenching vibration of the tears he was powerless to stop.

It hurt like hell to see her like this. He cared too damn much. As much as he'd ever cared. Dammit.

His thoughts easily transferred from her to the child she had carried for nine months. Every time he had thought of Mick today, his gut had clenched. Ever since she had told him of the cessation of her dream, he had feared what she feared.

Their son was dead.

He spoke with tenderness. "How's the shoulder?"

"It hurts."

"I guess I shouldn't have . . ." His lazy gaze traveled the length of her body.

"I have no regrets." She stroked his square jaw. "At least not about anything that's happened in the last two days. Coming to you yesterday morning was the smartest thing I've ever done."

She didn't talk like the woman who had broken off with him nine years earlier. She sounded like a woman who wanted to make things return to what they had been.

If he were perfectly honest with himself, rekindling what he'd once shared with Ava was exactly what he'd always wanted. Which pretty much explained why he had never been able to fall in love with another woman. "You expect me to believe that?" he asked.

"I may not have always told you the complete truth, but I swear on Mama's grave,

I've never lied to you."

If he stood there holding her another second he'd end up on top of her again. As much as he wanted to, finding Mick was more important. He kissed her slender hand. "I'm going to throw those steaks on the grill. We need to eat."

"And since I'm not taking the Vicodin, I would like a glass of wine, *garcon.*"

He gave her a cocky smile. "I don't know about that. If the wine makes you any more passionate, I'll have to check into the hospital for exhaustion."

She threw the sofa pillow at him.

"Just kidding," he said. "I like my women passionate."

"Your women?" she called as he walked into the kitchen. "As in plural?"

He liked the jealous inflection in her voice. "Of course. Surely it hasn't escaped your notice that I'm rich — and reasonably attractive. The babes fall at my feet." He cranked up the oven to its highest setting and tossed in a couple of russet potatoes, then he tore open the package of T-bones and poured bottled marinade on them.

"Is that why you carry around those hundred dollar bills? To impress the chicks?"

"Hey, it works!" He went out the back door to the small, brick-enclosed barbecue grill. He'd thought it incongruous with a vintage bungalow, but appreciated.

When he came back into the kitchen, he uncorked the merlot and poured her a glass. No wine for him. He still preferred beer. In longnecks, Texas style.

"I can never remember," he said, handing her the glass of wine, "if you chill red wine or white."

"White."

"Good." He sat next to her, settling a possessive hand on her bare knee. "The outfit looks good on you." He paused. "But not as good as you looked a few minutes ago. I like my women . . ." His simmering gaze rained over her. "Unclothed."

My women. There was only one woman for him. Ava was his woman. Even if he knew she would leave him again tomorrow, at least he had this one day with her.

And the night that lay ahead.

"Blake?"

"Um hum?" His arm snaked around her.

"Are you seeing anyone in particular?"

"No *one* in particular."

"I'm glad."

"What about you?"

She was silent for a moment. "I'm not sure how to answer that. I have been seeing someone. A doctor at work. But it's never advanced to - - -"

"To what we just did?"

"Exactly."

"I'm glad. Of course, I'd have to kill him."

She giggled. The melodious sound carried him back a decade or more. Laughter had been as much a part of their relationship as lovemaking. "Gotta check the steaks."

* * *

"I'm not an invalid," she told him across the kitchen table as they ate dinner. "I could have helped prepare the meal."

"You don't need to aggravate that wound. I'd rather not - - -"

"See the sight of my blood?"

"Exactly."

She could not believe the ease with which they had fallen back into the same steps they had trod with one another so many years ago. It was almost as if they had never separated. In so many ways she lamented the past nine years. They had been the loneliest years of her life. Had she not experienced them, though, she would not cherish the present so dearly.

Since his eyes had raked over her in the hospital room, every second was precious. Especially the lovemaking. "Steak's good."

"Thanks. How's the wine?"

She gave him a sultry gaze. "You may need to cut me off."

"Does that mean what I think it does?"

Her lips seductively nibbled at the rim of the wine glass as her lashes lifted. "Maybe."

"Next time, it'll be in the bed."

"On brand new, crispy sheets."

"You make that sound erotic."

"It's a way of speaking I adopt in the presence of a certain man."

"Quit looking at me like that. I've got to finish the steak. After all, I'll need my - - -"

"Strength."

Their eyes met and held. "My grandmother would call you a fast cookie."

She giggled again. "My grandmother — if she were alive and if she knew about my seductive proclivities — would call me a tart."

"Must have been some food fetishes back in their day."

She slowly chewed her steak. "Personally, I like meat."

He set down his fork. "You are one naughty girl."

With any other man, the blatant sexuality they shared would be nothing more than lust. With Blake, it was intrinsically interwoven into the fabric of their love.

Love? She was convinced without a doubt.

She wanted to tell him. She wanted to say, "I love you." She wanted to tell him she had never loved any man but him. But this was not the right time for such a declaration.

Despite the undeniable magnetism between them, she could not take his affection for granted. She had once trampled on it. He could not be expected to easily trust her again. Such trust must be earned.

Blake's cell phone rang. She glanced at her

watch. Quarter after nine.

He picked it up. "Tranowski."

He nodded, met her gaze, and said, "Get a piece of paper and write this down."

She rushed to her purse and fetched a pen and the first paper she could find, which happened to be her checkbook.

"Seventeen sixty-four Marigold Avenue."

Chapter 6

"That address you wrote down is Pacheco's residence. I'd like to do a drive-by to see if the slime balls who shot you are there." He strapped on his shoulder holster while she fetched her purse and slid into flip flops.

When they reached his pickup truck, he instructed her to don his baseball cap, an authentic one from the New York Yankees.

She pulled up her hair and tucked it beneath the hat while he backed out of the narrow driveway. "I, uh, saw your debut with the Yankees."

He tapped at the brakes, his jaw dropping. "You were in New York?"

"No. I saw the game at a Houston sports bar." She would not reveal how sad it had made her not to be sharing his big moment with him. They had both dreamed for so many years about him standing on the pitchers' mound at Yankee Stadium.

"And you knew I would be pitching that night because. . ."

"Because I went to the Yankees' website every morning to keep track of your career."

He was silent for a moment as he navigated out of the maze of short, residential streets that braided onto a boulevard which was a straight shot to the freeway. "So you saw my first and last game for the Yankees. The line-drive that shattered my kneecap that night put an end to my pitching career."

She knew enough about baseball to know that a pitcher's power came from the legs more than the arm.

"I was OK with it, really. I was never happy pitching out of the bullpen, and they'd pretty much told me I didn't have what it takes to be a starter."

"And being a starting pitcher was all you'd ever wanted," she said solemnly. "I suppose it was meant for you to be the best private investigator in the Lone Star state. At least that's what I've been told."

"Pete and I have been lucky. A couple of high profile cases, and we've got more business than we can handle. I'm lucky, too, to have had jobs that I love to go to every day."

"Not many men can say that."

Upon entering the freeway's on ramp, he accelerated. "What about you, Ava? You finding that cure for cancer you were dead set on finding?"

"We're certainly working on it."

"Who's *we*?"

"I'm a member of a research team at the

tumor institute."

"Then I guess we've both been lucky to be doing what we enjoy."

Her job had been fulfilling, but it was no replacement for all she had so foolishly given up. She wanted to tell Blake of her regrets, but this wasn't the time. The only thing that mattered now was Mick. "If you don't believe Walter Meecham would harm his adopted son, why do you think Mick has disappeared?" Somehow, she could not refer to Walter Meecham as Mick's father. Not without putting *adopted* in front of it.

"I wish to God I knew. If it were just the wife who had gone missing, I could understand it better. The woman was an heiress. If Meecham tired of her for whatever reason, he would lose her money, too. Unless she died."

The very word *died* sent Ava's stomach tumbling. "Do you think our son is . . ."

"Dead?" His hands gripped the steering wheel more tightly. "You have to be prepared for that possibility." His voice sounded as sorrowful as she felt. "Though I still believe Meecham cares about the kid."

She harrumphed. Blake hadn't met Walter Meecham.

The illuminated white dome of the state capital building shone in the night sky as they sped south on the freeway. "Let's go with your assumption that Meecham wants to be rid of the wife — but not the boy," she said. "Why are they both missing?"

"There has to be a logical explanation." Cruising along at the speed limit, Blake spoke as if he were reciting case notes into a Dictaphone. Then all of a sudden he slapped at the steering wheel. "I've got it!"

"What?"

"Mrs. Meecham's left him. I've allowed myself to buy into your theory that the kid's in danger when it's nothing more than marital discord."

Now she, too, felt hopeful. "That *might* explain why Mr. Meecham was so reluctant to discuss the disappearance."

"He's obviously a proud man, a private man."

"Who's angling for a reconciliation."

"Especially if she deprived him of the boy."

"That *could* explain why I have such a strong feeling that they're here in Austin."

His brows hiked. "Here we go again. You're having one of your feelings."

"Call it motherly instinct." That was the first time in eight years she had alluded to herself as a mother, a name she had long ago forfeited. "But I feel certain they aren't out of state. I believe they're in Austin."

"I feel the same, though I have nothing concrete to base it on." He exited the freeway and began to follow the navigation system's screen. "We should be getting fairly close now. In the dark, you can probably pass for a boy." He quickly glanced at her.

Did she really look like a boy? "Why not a man?"

"Too small."

She sat up taller. On the northwest quadrant of the screen she located Marigold Street. "You need to turn left at the second block we come to."

The houses on Marigold were few and far between, each of them surrounded by at least three acres of flat, treeless land and accessed by driveways that spanned a drainage ditch.

"Looks like the perfect hangout for criminals who don't want to arouse neighbors' suspicions," Blake said. "Can you read any addresses?"

"They're on the mailboxes." Like a lopsided appendage, lone mailboxes on posts faced the street at the base of each driveway. "This one's Seventeen Fifty-eight. Looks like Pacheco's house is on the same side of the street."

Blake dimmed his lights and eased off the accelerator.

"This is it," she said as they reached the next driveway. A filigree metal sign spelling "Rancho Grande" arched across the asphalt drive. Blake's pickup came to a complete stop as he and Ava peered at the sprawling one-story stucco house that, beneath the glow of a half a dozen flood lights, looked as if it had been painted with soft pink watercolors. There did not appear to be a garage, just a parking court in front — empty of cars.

"Looks like nobody's at Rancho Grande." Blake sounded disappointed. "Not a single vehicle, not a single light on in the house."

"I doubt anyone's gone to bed. It's not yet ten."

He nodded. "Looks like we go back to Evergreen Street and plan our next move."

He turned around in the next driveway.

Lulled by the inky darkness and the smooth hum of his vehicle, neither spoke for the next several moments. As much as Ava wanted to believe that Mrs. Meecham had taken Mick and walked away from her marriage, she could not. Not when every morsel of instinct she possessed told her the son she had given birth to was in danger. "Let's say Mrs. Meecham left her husband. Where would she go?" Ava asked. "Isn't that the kind of *What if?* you specialize in?"

Oncoming headlights flashed across his pensive face as he nodded. "When I'm called in, it's usually because the split's not amicable. In that case, the woman is usually afraid of her husband and goes into hiding."

"With friends or relatives?"

He shook his head. "Too obvious."

"Then to a hotel?"

"Sometimes, but that's pretty easy to track."

"Even with an alias?"

"To a man with Meecham's financial resources, yes."

"You mean he could have enough flunkies armed with photos combing local hotels and motels and questioning employees and guests?"

"Exactly."

"Then where would she go?"

"If she's planned to flee for a long time — and with her personal fortune — Elaine Meecham could have purchased a piece of property her husband doesn't know about."

"Can you find out?"

"I'll get on it as soon as we get back to the house."

* * *

The first thing he did when they got back was let his laptop boot up while he placed a call to Tiffany at home. "I need you and Tracie to start checking every hotel and motel in Austin for a fifty-eight-year-old white female named Elaine Meecham who should be accompanied by an eight-year-old boy named Mick. She's blond; his hair is dark. They quite possibly are using aliases. She drives a Mercedes, TDL number . . ." He pulled his smartphone from his pocket, pressed some buttons, and glanced at a column of notes before finishing, "GRS 728. You girls will get double time — and future days off — for this."

God, but he hoped Mrs. Meecham and

Mick were holed up in some hotel or some property she had purchased on the sly. It was *the* logical explanation for their disappearance.

But why in the hell did he share Ava's bad vibes about their whereabouts? Why did he, too, believe his son was in jeopardy?

"Don't you ever write anything down?" she asked.

"I learned a long time ago that I'm prone to losing slips of paper. That can be costly in my business."

"I just realized. . ." An astonished look flicked across her pretty face. "At your office. I didn't see any file cabinets or –"

"Paper?"

"Yes!"

"It's pretty much a paperless office. Everything is stored electronically, backed up endlessly, and accessible only by highly protected passwords."

"Then I could never work there. I have to write everything down."

"You'd get used to electronic data entry."

His attention turned to the laptop, where he keyed in Travis County properties. After a moment, he determined that Elaine Meecham had not purchased any property in that county. He checked his case notes on his smartphone again and paused when he came to Elaine Meecham's maiden name: Markowitz.

At the laptop, he punched in Elaine Markowitz. There were plenty of Markowitzes, but no Elaine listed as a property owner in Travis County.

Perhaps she had fled to a neighboring county. He tried Comal County. And struck out. Then he tried Bexar, the county where San Antonio was located. Like in Comal County, there was no property belonging to either Elaine Meecham or Elaine Markowitz.

He slumped back into his chair and sighed.

"So?" Ava asked.

"I don't think Elaine Meecham purchased property in her own name. At least not around Austin."

"Hopefully your Tiffany and Tracie will find something."

He was not hopeful. "There's still the fact that after you went poking around trying to locate Mick, those scumbags tried to kill you. The two have to be related. Which brings us back–"

"To Mick being in danger."

His eyes shut tightly, and he nodded. "I'm afraid so. Even if I don't believe Walter Meecham would harm the kid."

"What if — for reasons completely incomprehensible to us — Pacheco's gang is holding Mrs. Meecham and Mick?"

It was a possibility he would rather not contemplate. Pacheco's hired hands were seriously bad news. "I think I'll check out Pacheco's properties."

He started with Travis County. Pacheco obviously had a lot of money and could have property anywhere, but Blake was hoping the dirt bags and Pacheco's Hummer were still in Travis County. Hopefully at a house owned by Pacheco.

Thirty seconds later, a list of Carlos Pachecos scrolled down his screen. "I had no idea there were so many Carlos Pachecos living in Travis County."

"It's a big place."

"Too bad I don't know his middle name."

"Is there some way you could get it from his criminal record?"

"Maybe so." He closed that window on his computer and went to the URL for the Travis County District Clerk. "Wish I had the exact birth date for Pacheco."

"He's forty-three, if that helps any."

He looked up at her. "How did you know that?"

"It was in the newspaper article. Of course, I haven't a clue as to his birthday."

"The forty-three will help."

Working with criminal data bases was one of his specialties. Three minutes later, he hit pay dirt. "Got it!"

She looked over his shoulder at the computer screen. Carlos Miguel Pacheco. "Apparently he's an American citizen," Blake said. "Born in Laredo. Laredo, Texas." The Marigold address was listed for his residence, and he was apparently single. These statistics were followed by a lengthy criminal history.

"Then he's an American citizen," she whispered.

"It looks like it."

Blake went back to the property records and clicked on the name Carlos Miguel Pacheco.

A long list of properties trailed down the screen. "I'll start calling these out to you."

"Let me get something to write on."

"I've got that covered." He took his phone from his jeans pocket and went to the map function. A couple of menu options later, he handed the phone to her. "You can type the addresses here, starting with his home address."

As he called them out, she entered the address on Marigold Street, then each of the thirteen other addresses.

He pointed at one of the addresses listed on his laptop. "This one is land only. See? I think we can exclude those. We're definitely looking for a building."

She copied down every one. All fourteen of them. "I don't think you could ever change my mind set. I'd always want to write things down."

He fleetingly wondered how long they would stay together this time. He did not like to think about losing her a second time.

There was merit in the idea of nipping this whole thing in the bud — all in the interest of saving him from future pain. Sort of like chopping off a gangrened leg to save a life.

"Let's go," she said, sliding her purse strap over her good shoulder.

"Go where?"

"To every last building owned by Carlos Miguel Pacheco. We've got to find Mick."

"Not yet."

He took the phone and programmed it to map the addresses into an efficient route. Then he hit the speed dial for Pete.

"Alvarez."

"You still got friends on the Austin PD?"

"One or two. Why?"

"I need you to see if they've had any luck finding the guys driving the Hummer today."

"I'll see what I can learn. Anything else?"

"Yeah. I've got Tiff and Tracie calling every hotel and motel in Austin trying to locate Elaine Meecham and her son, who are missing. Can you get Dave to start checking parking lots at hotels and motels for her late-model Mercedes, GRS 728?"

"No need. It's in the garage at the Meecham's residence."

"Damn!"

"Nothing much is going on there. He's watching the Spurs on TV. Gotta be a great guy."

Pete loved the San Antonio Spurs.

"Let me know if you learn anything." Blake terminated the call and turned to Ava. "The cap goes back on once we hit the truck."

As they drove through the sparse late-night traffic, Blake said, "My hunch — and that's all it is, a hunch — is that *if* these thugs did have the Meecham woman and Mick they wouldn't be holding a woman and child at a private residence. I think they'd wait until dark and then take them to a commercial building located in an area where there's no activity at night."

"That seems plausible. I recognized a couple of street names as being in more industrialized area of the city. In fact, they were both in the same area of east Austin."

"Let's start there, then."

That particular area of East Austin wasn't the kind of neighborhood he wanted to be in after dark, and he sure as hell wouldn't have come with Ava had he known it was this rough looking. There were a couple of metal-roofed cantinas, an abundance of used tire shops, and plenty of shacks — they couldn't be called houses — where air conditioning was clearly not available, judging from the bare chested men sitting on sagging front porches as they tossed down brews.

"What block is this?" he asked.

"Thirteen hundred."

"It should be in the next block. Fourteen

twenty-nine."

He had stopped at the stop sign at the end of the thirteen hundred block. Not that he wanted to. He didn't like this neighborhood at all. Once again, he pressed the power locks.

If it were just him, he wouldn't be so nervous, but being responsible for Ava's safety was another matter. He still could not dislodge the horrifying memory of seeing that shaved-headed bastard level his gun at her, could not forget the horror that gripped him when looked into her car and saw all that blood.

"It's going to be on the left side," she said.

He slowed as he drew closer to the address. There were no signs of life in this block. First building on the right, a boarded up *taqueria.* Next, a narrow building, obviously closed now, with a flaking, unreadable sign. Next, a wider property that featured a four-car bay connected to a small, old stucco building. The rear of the property was enclosed with a chain-link fence. *Ramirez Paint & Body.*

But he could not find its address. He drove slowly past it. The sign on the next building was not illuminated, but the letters were big enough and the block's lone street light allowed him to read *Ofelia's Palm Reading.* Below that, fourteen thirty-four.

They'd gone too far. It must be the paint and body. He swerved his big pickup into a U and headed back. "It's the paint and body shop."

"Any lights on?"

"Nope." He eased his truck into the paved drive in front of the business. "You stay here. And stay down!"

"If no one's there who could recognize me - - -"

"I'll determine if no one's there. Give me the flashlight from the glove box."

He shoved it in his pocket as he got out of the truck. Each of the bays was secured with horseshoe locks and chains, as was the front door of the small building. Next, he tried the lock which secured the gate. No go there, either.

Time to try his skeleton key. Might as well go for the front door. If the Meecham woman and Mick were here, they'd likely be in the building adjacent to the body shop.

Sixty seconds later, he was entering the building, his gun drawn. No sounds. Which convinced him this was not the place where the boy was.

Only a partial wall separated this office area from the actual garage where the body work was done. He strolled into that area and flipped on his flashlight. A triangle of yellow light shone on over a pair of low-slung vintage cars that were in the process of being customized.

He projected the light toward the back.

There was a room like an oven, big enough to toast a car, outfitted with high power light coils.

This was obviously a working business. Hardly a place where a woman and kid would be kept.

He returned to the truck. "No luck."

"You're sure?"

"Yeah, it looks like work's being done here by day."

He depressed the master door lock and started the truck. A few minutes later he turned left. Divided by a median, this highway looked more like what he was hoping for. No residences. A lot of industrial type business where no one would be around at night. Unless they were up to no good.

"The next address is on the first major cross street we come to. Looks like we go down about a mile and turn back to the left."

"Address?"

Her gaze dropped to the phone's illuminated screen. "One, six, thirteen."

"See if you can make out any of these addresses. It's really dark here." Street lights were few and far between, and there were no cars behind him. No Hummers, either, thank God. She glanced to her right. A moment later, she said, "I finally see one. Slow down." Her eyes narrowed. "OK, this is one, two, eighteen."

"Then it'll be on my side, up about four

blocks." But since he had not come to a single cross street, he wondered if the street numbering here would follow normal patterns. These properties stretched over a lot of real estate. They could be taking up city blocks that weren't here. "See if you can make out one more address." He slowed, and the van behind him swung into the left lane to pass him.

A minute later she said, "That business has a nice sign! Let's get your headlights on it."

He slowed down enough that the arc of his lights shone on the six-inch high numbers on a brick planter. "One, six, twenty-two."

"Good. It should be close. On the left."

A fairly short distance away — on the left side of the road — a large metal building was set back from the road about a hundred yards. "That may be it," he mused, turning into a lane that led up to the building.

If he were going to hide someone, this would be the kind of place he would choose. It looked as if a few fenced acres of industrial equipment surrounded the warehouse. No close neighbors.

He cut off his headlights.

He was expecting occupation. And wished like hell he hadn't brought Ava.

As he drove closer to the warehouse, he took note of a gate to its side. Chain link.

Beyond it, a parked car. Some kind of

muscle car. Like a Mustang. But he couldn't make it out in the dark.

"Someone's here," he said. "Get down. On the floorboard."

He pulled to a stop and cut off the engine. "You're to stay here. We may have found something." He drew his weapon. "Don't get out of the truck, no matter what." He tossed her the keys. "Got the phone?"

"Yes," she answered, her voice thin.

"Call the police if you need to." His hand gripped the door handle, then he paused and spoke firmly. "If you have any reason to believe I've met with trouble, get the hell out of here." As he eased open the door, he ordered her to lock it behind him.

Her heart thumping, she stayed crouched down in the black hole of his truck. They couldn't have picked a darker night. She wished she had asked him what he had seen, what had made him so concerned for her safety. Was this the place where poor little Mick was?

Several minutes passed. That she'd heard nothing was a good sign. At least Blake hadn't endangered himself.

Just as she was settling into a semi-comfort zone, she heard a shot.

A single shot some distance away.

She involuntarily screamed. Blake? Mick? She went to leave the truck, but remembered Blake's last warning to her.

Fear pounding into every pore of her, she prayed that Blake had not been killed.

Still huddled low in his truck, she braced for the sound of more bullets. She had learned all too painfully that morning that bullets came in groups.

But after a way-too-lengthy wait, she realized there were not going to be any more gunshots.

That had to mean someone had surprised Blake. And killed him. One shot, one kill. They must have aimed the gun at his head.

A feeling of grief consumed her. After all these years of loneliness, and especially after what they had rekindled that night, she had come to realize how important Blake was to her. How necessary. If he were dead, she had no desire to live. She pulled herself up and yanked open the pickup's door.

Though the building's entry had obviously been forced open, its door was now closed. She strode through the doorway into complete darkness. Easing the door closed behind her, she stopped and listened intently. No sound whatsoever.

Too bad she had no flashlight. The long, dark hallway she began to walk along reminded her of the one in her dream. Her stomach flipped. This had to be the place where her baby was, the place from where he called to her night after night.

And, by God, she was going to find him!

She inched open the first door she came to. Not that she could see a darn thing. She flipped on an overhead light. The room was lined with towering metal shelves that stored spools of cable.

In order for the light from that storage room to illuminate the dark central hallway, she had to manipulate the arm at the top of its door.

In the next room she found more cable.

She bypassed the next couple of doors, suspecting that what she was looking for was at the end of the long corridor. Like in her dream.

The gunshots had not sounded close. The very thought of gunshots convinced her Blake was dead. She felt like the walking dead herself. As she covered more distance, her light source grew more dim. Darkness thickened until she was once again surrounded by darkness. Just like in her dream.

She stumbled over something, falling to her knees, catching herself with her hands. Her palms slickened with moisture.

Blake's blood. She had fallen over his body. Tears sliding down her cheeks, her heart hammering, she got to her feet and went to the nearest side room, flicking on the light and dreading what she would see.

She turned and opened her tightly shut eyes. There, sprawled in the hallway was a shaved-headed twenty-something, a revolver in his hand, a bullet wound in his head.

Blake was still alive!

She proceeded down the hall which terminated at a steel door. A closed steel door. Just like in her dream. She drew her breath and opened the door.

Gun drawn, Blake leaned over a slender woman with whitish hair. A river of blood pooled next to her lifeless body.

It was Elaine Meecham.

Chapter 7

At Ava's horrifying scream, Blake jerked around.

She stood frozen at the doorway, her shocked gaze lifting from the dead woman to Blake, her eyes sorrowful. "Mrs. Meecham?"

His lashes lowered, he nodded.

"Why did you kill her?"

"I found her like this."

"And. . . Mick?" Her voice quivered.

"He's not here. I've looked everywhere."

She began to whimper, the soft ebb of tears glistening on her cheeks. "D–d-did you kill the guy back there?"

He would rather not talk about it. He wished to God he hadn't had to shoot the kid. But he'd had no choice. "It was him or me." The wannabe thug didn't even look old enough to buy beer.

"So that was the shot I heard?"

A spark of anger flashed in his eyes. "I told you not to leave the truck."

"I thought you were dead."

"So you should have gotten the hell out of here."

"Why?" she asked, her voice forlorn. "If you were dead, I wouldn't want to live."

If she had said anything else, he could have stayed angry.

Never removing his gaze from her, he reholstered his gun and went to her, drawing her into his arms. Powerful emotions rocketed through him. Despite that he'd just killed a guy, despite that they stood just feet from the bloodied body of his son's adoptive mother, despite the nausea rising in his belly, nothing had ever felt better than standing there holding Ava Simpson in his arms.

But he had to pull away, had to get her out of here.

Gently weeping, she clung to him like a barnacle. "Mickey will be next."

He lifted her chin with a knuckle. "I'll do everything in my power to prevent that from happening."

Her weeping turned to sobs. Wrenching sobs.

"We've got to get out of here," he said. "Now. We barely missed meeting her fate ourselves." Though the dead hoodlum could have killed the Meecham woman, he suspected others had been there. Others who had taken Mick away.

"How do you know that?" Her anguished face lifted.

"Because her blood's fresh."

Ava shivered."Was she shot?"

"No. Her throat was slashed."

She gasped and turned away from the bloody sight of Elaine Meecham's lifeless body. "You really have hope that Mickey's all right?"

"I'll tell you what I think once we're out of here."

Something on top of an upturned milk crate caught her eye, and she walked to it.

As soon as he saw what it was, his heart caught. "A Game Boy electronic game."

She flicked it on. It was a baseball game. "Mick's been here. Oh, dear God, the poor child must have seen his mother murdered."

"The sons of bitches!"

"Whoever killed Mrs. Meecham must have taken Mick. We have to call the police!"

That had been his first thought when he found the Meecham woman's body. Now that they had proof — and not just Ava's crazy dreams — that Mick was in danger they could go to the police.

But after finding the Game Boy, Blake was convinced his son's life was in jeopardy. "First, we're going to get the hell out of here."

They returned to the truck, and he could not get off the property fast enough.

"Where are we going?" she asked once he was back on the highway.

"To our place."

* * *

In fifteen minutes they were back at the

bungalow, and he was pouring Ava a glass of wine. "This might help to steady your nerves."

He could have injected a quart of whiskey straight into his own veins. Already upset over having to kill a fellow human being, now he was reeling from the almost-certainty that his son's life was in the hands of murderers.

He downed a bottle of beer quickly.

"I think you may have been right," she said.

"About what?"

"About Walter Meecham. He had his wife killed. For her money. And he's spared Mick's life."

"I know I've never met the guy, never had a conversation with him about his son, but I've had a hunch from the very beginning that he's an especially doting father. From what I've learned, he never had any children until he decided to adopt Mick when he was fifty-seven. Records show he insisted on a boy."

"And other things seem to point to the fact that the child has been nurtured."

He crossed the room and tossed his bottle into a trash can. "It's just a little thing, but the fact that he was involved in Little League sports tells me his adoptive parents wanted him to be a well-rounded kid. I just have this strong feeling they really love him. A lot." He paused, his lips compressed. "But I'm no longer so sure about Mick's safety. If the kid witnessed his mother's brutal murder, he can identify the perps."

"We'll have to call in the police. We've got to find him."

"I'm afraid. What if the police mess up?"

There was resignation in her voice when she said, "If the police mess up, the gang members will kill Mickey."

In a time of tremendous stress, she had chosen to call their child Mickey. He liked it. It suited his vision of the boy. His son.

"That's my fear. Someone as powerful as Pacheco is bound to have cops on his payroll. What if someone in Austin PD tips them off?"

"Then our son could be killed."

"We have to find Mick. I think we're on the right track with the property rolls."

"I do, too."

"And with Pete's help, we have a chance of being able to rescue the poor kid."

She sipped her wine thoughtfully. "Then we need to keep checking Carlos Pacheco's properties."

"Not we."

She moved to him, stood on her toes and brushed soft lips against his. "If you're going to die, Blake Simon Tranowski, I have to go with you."

He didn't know if she was telling him the truth or telling him what she thought he wanted to hear. But no words had ever sounded more romantic. They sort of made *I love you* sound wimpy. His arms closed around her, and he held her tightly. "I vowed to keep you safe."

"I don't want safe, I want you."

He hardened instantly. But he wouldn't act upon it. Not while their son's life held in the balance.

His cell phone rang. He extracted himself from her clinginess and punched the Talk button. "Tranowski."

"I've got something really interesting," Pete said.

"About Meecham?"

"Oh, yeah. I was able to hack into his cell phone records, and guess who he's been talking to? A lot."

"Well, it can't be Pacheco."

"But it's the closest thing to Pacheco. His half brother, Julio Estrada. My sources tell me Estrada's running the operation while his brother's in jail."

Why in the hell was a successful businessman like Walter Meecham hooking up with such lowlifes? And how in the hell were he and Ava going to go up against such an organization to find their son? "You have his whereabouts?"

"Possibly. Got something to write with?"

"Just a sec." Blake's glance whisked to Ava. "Get something to write this down."

She rushed to her purse and whipped out her checkbook and a pen.

"I'll give you everything I've got," Pete said.

"Name: Julio Juan Estrada. DOB two, seventeen, sixty-seven. Home address, twelve ninety-two South Freemont."

"Is the guy married?"

"Yeah, but his wife lives in Laredo. He's got a mistress in Austin who resides at the Freemont address."

"Any kids around?"

"Nope."

"Vehicle?"

"Another Hummer."

"And I'll bet it's black."

"That info I don't have."

"Criminal record?"

"You got an hour?"

"That long, huh?"

"Last arrest four years ago. Success spawns good attorneys — and flunkies to do their dirty work."

"That, too. Listen, I need to get one of guys to stake out another address." Blake gave Pete the address of the warehouse where the two dead bodies were located. "I need to know everything about anyone who comes or goes at that address. And it's imperative that our guy not be spotted."

"What's going on?" Pete's voice was heavy with concern.

"Serious stuff."

There was a long pause. "Like murder?"

"Yeah."

"You need to call the police."

"Can you guarantee me there's not a single officer on the Austin PD who's not on Pacheco's payroll?"

"You know I can't. But what's your stake in this, Blake?"

Blake drew a deep breath. "I can't fill you in on everything right now, but I will tell you that a little boy who's very important to me is being held by the bastards. The child may have witnessed his mother's brutal murder."

"I'm coming to Austin."

"Good." Blake's voice softened. "You've got to understand that the child must be safely extricated from these cut-throats."

"We'll give it our best shot."

"Call me when you reach Austin."

After he hung up, Ava gave him a puzzled look. "Why didn't you tell him about the deaths?"

"The less people who know, the safer Mickey will be." He had to play to her fears.

"I need to fill you in on what Pete said." He topped off her wine glass, then came to sit beside her, frowning.

"What?"

"Meecham's cell records show he's been in frequent communication with Pacheco's half brother, Julie Estrada, who's running the organization."

"Good lord!"

He booted up his laptop. "I'm going to check property records for Estrada, too. If

Pacheco has extensive real estate holdings, my guess is, Estrada does, too."

He sat there at the kitchen table and keyed in the Travis Country Appraisal District rolls, Ava's chin resting on his shoulder as she stood behind him.

"You're one smart fella," she said when a lengthy list of properties owned by Julio Juan Estrada — including the one on South Freemont — scrolled down the screen.

Without being told, she took out the phone and began to feed in the addresses. "We've certainly got our work cut out for us."

He shut off the laptop and stretched. "I can't figure out why they kept a guy posted back there, guarding the body."

"I think I know. It was obvious that the warehouse is a hub of commercial activity. Daytime activity. Did you notice that last room — the one where Mrs. Meecham was slain — was soundproofed?"

He had seen the heavy padding on the walls which indicated to him that both Mrs. Meecham and the boy had likely been held there for several days. He understood what she was getting at. "We need to go back and put the guy's body in the same room as Mrs. Meecham. We can't take the chance on some legitimate employee finding it when he comes to work in the morning."

"But what if they send a replacement for the dead guy? Tonight?"

"I have a feeling he was hunkered down for a long shift. The kitchen there was pretty well stocked."

"In case we don't find Mickey at one of the properties tonight we need to make sure someone showing up at the warehouse tomorrow morning doesn't find the bodies."

"We've got a helluva a lot to do before daylight. Pete can help. He's on his way to Austin."

"Good."

"How many buildings under Estrada's ownership?"

She looked back at the phone. "Only five."

"Can you tell which are not in residential areas?"

She read over them once more, then shrugged. "I'm not sure. Four of the addresses I'm pretty sure are in commercial areas. One of them I believe to be rural."

He hadn't thought of rural. That sounded especially promising. The only problem was that they could spend their precious hours before daylight commuting to the country on a wild goose chase. "You got any hunches?" he asked.

"My first instinct is to go rural, but it could be more than an hour away. I'm afraid we don't have that kind of time. Especially if we're to go back and put that dead guy in the room with Mrs. Meecham." She glanced over the addresses once more. One of the street names she remembered from the navigation system map earlier in the evening. "Actually, this address on Heffington is close to the paint and body shop."

"Then we'll check it out when we go back to the warehouse."

* * *

Nothing would have been more horrifying than stumbling over Blake's dead body in the dark, but a close second was discovering poor Mrs. Meecham — graceful Mrs. Meecham — sprawled lifeless, hideous amounts of blood obscuring the elegant neck which had once so beautifully displayed a diamond choker.

Now Mickey's mother was gone. Ava would never have given him up had she thought he would be deprived of a mother's tender love.

She hoped like hell poor Mickey had not seen his mother's brutal murder, hoped he would never have to learn of the cruel manner in which she lost her life. Most of all, she hoped Mick was safe.

Blake grabbed his keys and turned to her. "Are you sure you're up to going? You've got to be in a lot of pain."

He had that right. The shoulder pain that had been throbbing all night had intensified in the past half hour. Even the thought of moving her arm hurt. But she had no intentions of sharing that information with him. She would minimize her activities and do her best to keep Blake from knowing how much pain she was in. "I have to go with you. You know that."

Chapter 8

It was a good thing Blake had remembered to bring towels. After he dragged Skinhead into the back room with Mrs. Meecham's body, he set about to clean up the blood that had pooled around the body and trailed into that back room. He only wished he'd brought more towels.

Turning on a bright light had posed no threats because the metal building had no windows. He even lucked out and found cleaning supplies in a closet. As he swished the mop over the site, his mind raced. If someone got alarmed by being unable to reach the dead dude on his cell, that could spell disaster. Or if the guy's body were discovered early tomorrow, that, too, could alert Estrada's bunch that someone besides Meecham might know about the kid's abduction.

And what incentive would there be to keep the boy alive then?

For now, he must hope no one would try to reach the dead guy tonight, and no one would see anything suspicious when they entered the building the next morning.

Most of all, he hoped he'd find the kid before morning.

Time, though, was as big an enemy as Carlos Pacheco's murdering gang. There weren't enough hours of dark left to check out every address on their list. Even if he and Ava split up. Which he wasn't about to do. He was not going to let her out of his sight until every last member of their gang was incarcerated.

When he returned to his truck and saw that Ava was all right, a feeling of relief swished over him like a warm wave. She had insisted on staying in the truck as a watcher and had agreed to call his cell if anyone else happened on the scene. Even though he hadn't wanted to leave her unprotected for a moment, he had to admit it was a good plan.

"Where to next?" he asked his navigator.

"To Estrada's place on South Freemont."

* * *

The time on his dash said it was quarter to midnight. She was not used to staying up this late, but she'd slept well the night before. So why in the heck did she feel so rotten? The worst kind of fatigue had set in. The kind that made your bones ache, made your mind dull.

No way could she sleep, though. She and Blake were committed to staying up all night, searching every last one of these addresses until they found Mickey. Surely he had to be held at one of the properties.

Trouble was, if they looked all night, there still wouldn't be enough time to make it to every property in Travis County that was owned by Estrada or Pacheco.

Ten minutes later they were searching for street numbers on a row of tightly packed storefronts on a street that had probably seen its heyday three quarters of a century earlier. "I see one!" She began to call out, "Forty-seven, twenty-nine."

"Then it should be in the next block."

The next block was lined on both side of the streets with cars and pickups. "Something's happenin' around this place."

She was pretty sure the "happenin'" was occurring at the bar in the middle of the block. A blinking neon sign identified it as Joe's Bar. Joe didn't seem like a name that would be used in this predominately Hispanic neighborhood. But the sign did look pretty old. Mid-nineteen hundreds. Before Hispanic immigrants had moved into the area. "What number we looking for?"

"Four eight five two," she said.

"My side. Help me look."

"I think it's the bar."

"I don't guess it's got a second story?"

"Nope."

"Then this can't be the place we're looking for. What's next?"

She punched buttons for the next couple

of blocks. "The next closest place is a couple of miles away. On Highway 183. Come down here a couple of more lights until you come to 183 and turn right."

Highway 183 was another divided highway lined principally with commercial buildings. "Address?" he asked.

"One zero three ten."

"Can you tell which way we're going? Up or down?"

She sighed. "There don't seem to be any addresses."

"I thought the postal service wasn't supposed to deliver mail to any address that was not clearly indicated."

"These businesses must have a postman who looks the other way. Oh! Slow down. I see something."

He eased up on the accelerator as they coasted by a now-closed ice cream shop.

"One zero one, one, one."

"Guess we're a couple of blocks away."

"And it will be on your side of the street."

The second block they came to was taken up by a horseshoe-shaped, flat-roofed shopping center that looked as if it had been constructed in the 1960's. Its U curved around a large – and surprisingly full – parking lot. More flashing neon lights proclaimed this to be Monterrey Ballroom. "Pretty surprising crowd here for a weekday night," he said. He pulled in. "Anything else here besides the ballroom?"

"Nothing that's open this time of night. Why don't we just drive along the sidewalk part?"

A sidewalk ran along the perimeter of the U, formerly linking all the stores. But she suspected the popularity of the Monterrey Ballroom had swallowed up the surrounding shops.

"I don't see anything else," she said.

"It's one helluva big ballroom."

"And loud."

"Are you thinking what I'm thinking?"

"That cries for help wouldn't be heard?"

He skidded his truck to a stop, then slid into one of the few remaining parking places. "Exactly. Let's check it out."

"I'm not dressed for dancing."

"Who said we're going to dance?"

A line of about ten couples stood waiting to get in the ballroom's main entrance, which was located in the direct middle of the old shopping center. "Let's unobtrusively meander around to the back." So, like her, he still couldn't shake the fear that the thugs from the parking lot would recognize them.

Seven or eight metal back doors gave onto the rear alley. They would all be locked.

"I'd feel better if I'd left you secure in the truck, but I don't like having you out of my sight, either."

The fact that he worried over her — which

surely meant he cared, didn't it? — would have made her smile if she weren't so damned worried about Mick, weren't feeling so damned tired, weren't feeling so damn much pain. It took a few minutes for him to get into the first door. The light from his flashlight fanned over an empty room. Completely empty. What a waste. Estrada wasn't stupid enough to keep anything that pointed to his illegal activities at a property that was legally under his ownership.

The drumbeat of contemporary Latin music vibrated the building, but the sounds were not as loud as they would be were the dance floor or bandstand on the other side of the wall from this last space. He would guess even the next space was unused. Either could have served to keep hostages.

Her pulse accelerated. "Let's try the next."

Now that he knew how to compromise the locks, he got into the next space more easily. Although it was dark like the other, it was not empty. The wand of light from his flashlight revealed Christmas decorations of every kind. Boxes of them. Giant plastic Santas. Faded red rubber bells bigger than beach balls. He shook his head. "Let's try the next."

But before he even tried the next lock, the high volume of the music told them this would take him directly into the Monterrey Ballroom.

"We don't want to go there," she said.

Just as they were moving away, the next door opened, and a young man in black came out. Blake pinned Ava against the brick wall and crushed his lips into hers. She instantly realized why and started to respond by enclosing her arms around his broad back. But she couldn't. The slightest movement of her injured shoulder triggered an almost unbearable pain.

The guy in black lit up a cigarette.

They surely couldn't stand here making out for the entire five minutes it would take the guy to smoke! No matter how satisfactory it was.

And no matter how seriously Blake was taking the subterfuge. Her little body molded to his, and she eagerly opened her mouth to the probe of his tongue.

"You little tart," he whispered.

"You fast cookie."

Apparently, the guy in black didn't relish the role of voyeur. After just a few puff of his cigarette, he threw it aside his and stomped it out before heading back into the blaring building.

The next three doors almost certainly led to the busy ballroom. He strode straight to the last two. When he reached the first of them, he put an ear to the door, then he picked the lock. Still no noise. He eased the door open, shining his flashlight into the room. There was but one thing in the room: a huge, brightly painted sign in red, white, and green that said *Cinco de Mayo*.

That left one last door, and she was losing all hope. When he reached it, he put ear to the door and listened before proceeding to pick the lock. Still no stirring. Index finger pressed to his lips, he faced Ava before sweeping open the door, the arc of light from his flashlight illuminating still-another empty room. "We've struck out."

Ava had never felt more dejected. "What I don't understand is why if they've got all these properties and businesses as successful as the Monterrey Ballroom, they still delve into illegal activities."

"Good question."

She started to round the corner, to head back toward the sprawling parking lot from the west.

He tugged at her. "I'd rather go back the way we came. Less exposure."

"Maybe we should go the rural route," she said when they reached the truck.

"The problem with that idea is that if we strike out, we will have wasted over two hours on the commute alone, not to even factor in the time searching the property."

"And time's something we don't have." She turned the air conditioning vents away from her. Once the sun went down, they didn't need the AC blaring. The cab of his truck was freezing! "Continue down 183. We'll hang a left at Oakside."

"How much farther do you think?"

"It's hard to say. Maybe a couple of miles."

They went at least another mile, and she was still chilled. She started to ask him to turn down the temperature, but the words stuck in her throat. It wasn't the air conditioning that was making her shiver.

It was fever!

Her thoughts flew back to the doctor's words that morning. She was to return to the hospital immediately at any sign of a fever.

But that she could not do. They could not afford to lose a single moment.|

No way could she allow Blake to know of her fever. He would insist on taking her to the hospital. He might even insist on staying there with her, losing valuable time that he could have spent looking for Mickey.

Besides, she was a trained nurse, for goodness sake. She knew how to deal with fevers. The trick was to do so without Blake becoming suspicious. "See if you can stop at a convenience store. The shoulder's bothering me. I'll just need to grab a Coke to take the ibuprofen with."

"You've got ibuprofen?"

"I always carry it in my purse."

"That purse of yours is a lethal weapon. You could knock someone out with it."

"Better that than a gun. Guns terrify me. But I'm glad you've got one tonight."

They drove past Oakside and still had not come to a convenience store. "Oakside's mostly residential, so I don't think we'll find a convenience store there."

She zoomed back on the navigation system screen. "We should be coming to Oltorff in a few more miles. I think we'll find something there."

It was nearly one a.m. when they reached a well-lit convenience store on busy Oltorff. Why couldn't she be one of those people who could swallow aspirins and such without liquid? They had wasted all this time just looking for her something to drink. By the time they got back to Oakside, they would have wasted a good twenty minutes. Twenty minutes they didn't have to waste.

She prayed Blake would not notice that she was shivering. At least she had darkness on her side. Now, if only she could get by without having to speak. Her teeth had begun to chatter.

He brought the cola to the passenger side, and she opened the door to take it. "You sure you're OK?" he asked.

"Sure." One syllables were manageable, but she dare not drink while he was so close.

"No signs of fever?"

"Nope." Why wouldn't he get back in the car? She needed his mind otherwise occupied.

He closed her door and circled the truck to

get back in the driver's seat.

After they were heading back toward Oakside, he asked, "You tired? It's late, and it's been a long day. Not to mention that you've got to be in a helluva a lot of pain. Maybe I should take you home."

"No." She didn't trust her chattering teeth to allow her to tell him all the reasons why she couldn't go home. She liked to think she was of some help. He could not have driven through these darkened neighborhoods, tried to make out street numbers, and navigate without her assistance. And taking her back to central Austin would eat up more precious minutes. A lot of them.

She tried to give him the impression the navigation system was sucking all her interest. She tried to ignore the stabbing, debilitating shoulder pain that ripped into every cell in her body and made her feel as if a sledge hammer were pounding into her scalp.

Surely the ibuprofen would kick in any minute and help to lower her temperature, help to take the edge off her screaming pain.

As they drew closer to their targeted neighborhood, her chills disappeared. They were replaced by waves of heat that began to soak her. She felt as if she could throw off her clothes and plunge into Barton Springs naked.

Every muscle in her body ached. A bed

sounded blissful. She'd like to lay on a bed covered in sheets wrung with ice water. With a whirling ceiling fan over the bed. And, God, but she wanted to sleep.

But not as much as she wanted — needed — to find Mickey.

"You're mighty quiet," Blake said.

She was thankful the chattering had stopped. "I've got my job to perform. I'm busy looking for street numbers. You'd think the city of Austin could afford more street lights. Don't they know well-lit streets discourage crime?"

"It's been my observation the better lit streets seem to be in the more affluent neighborhoods."

Even without good lighting, she could tell this residential area was far from affluent. If the houses had garages at all, they were single car. Front porches featured old sofas, and neatly trimmed lawns were nonexistent. In the daylight, she knew, they'd look potently shabby, but a peculiar peace washed over these totally dark bungalows of another era in the quiet of night. "I see an address!"

He slowed down. "Sixty-seven, ninety-one."

"And the address we're looking for?" he asked.

"Seventy-three, zero four."

"Six more blocks."

Each successive block they came to was less depressed than the last, the houses spreading out on wider, tree-dotted lots.

When they reached the seventy-three hundred block, Blake exclaimed, "Well, I'll be damned! Looks like your old friends are here."

She craned her neck.

And saw a black Hummer.

Chapter 9

"Don't even think about stopping," she said.

He slowed down.

She wished he wouldn't have. She was terrified of those guys. They should be asleep, darn it. It was after midnight. It was a week night, for crying out loud! Why was a light still shining in their window? They were probably watching television, not looking out the window or watching every vehicle that drove down their street. And even if they were looking out the window — which reason told her they could not be doing — what would they see? It was dark. Really dark.

"Get down!" Blake ordered.

Her heartbeat thumped. Had the shaved-headed guys walked out? She wasn't going to stick around to see. Those creeps seriously scared her. "Are they coming?" she asked from her huddled position on the floorboard.

"No. I'm just being prophylactic."

"Well, you scared me to death. Almost."

"It's pretty late for the lights to still be on."

No kidding, Sherlock. "We should get out of

here."

"What if the kid's there?"

"If those guys had been charged with keeping Mickey they wouldn't have been in a position to follow me this morning. My hunch — and you've got to admit my hunches are pretty accurate — is that other guys are watching Mickey."

"You're probably right, but we can't afford to leave any stone unturned."

"This is the last stone I want turned up."

"Sorry, babe. I really am."

He turned left at the next corner, then another quick left before dousing his lights and rolling to a complete stop. "You stay here. Don't poke your head up for any reason. Don't unlock the doors for anyone. I've got my own key." He opened the driver's side door. "And, for God's sake, use your cell if you have to."

"You're going to that house, aren't you?"

"I have to."

She couldn't argue. Still, she didn't like it. "Oh, Blake, I wish you wouldn't. Those guys *know* you. They've got guns."

"So do I."

"Yeah, but you're just one. They're two. Minimum."

"Quit worrying. I don't plan on letting them see me." He moved to get out.

"Blake?"

He turned back.

"I just want you to know something."

"What?"

"I love you."

"You shouldn't have had that second glass of wine." Then he exited the truck, easing the door closed almost noiselessly, and walked into the night made even darker beneath the heavy limbs of a spreading oak.

* * *

When Blake reached the block where he'd seen the Hummer, his first concern was to avoid rousing yapping dogs; so, he skimmed along the perimeter of the neighboring properties, thankful there were no streetlights here. His eye never left that lone lighted window until he came to the Hummer.

He used the vehicle for cover while he edged his way up to the house. Like a cat on soft paws, he angled into the overgrown ligustrum hedge that rimmed the house's front wall, then he squeezed between the bushes and the wall's exterior brick. Creeping cautiously, he moved toward what he presumed to be the living room, the room where the thugs from the parking garage must be gathered.

Spanish exclamations like the cheering at a soccer match greeted him. What in the hell was going on in that room? There were more than two men's voices, he was pretty sure. And he was pretty sure he was not mistaking their voices for the TV.

As he neared the window, his pulse clanged with fear. He'd never before done this kind of surveillance.

The kind that could get a guy killed.

But he'd never before had a case where a little boy's life was in jeopardy. Mick was worth the risk.

Gun drawn, he took a deep breath, then pressed his face to the window. Their backs to Blake, four youthful skinheads were squatted on the floor, rolling dice. They were playing craps. And so involved in the game, they weren't about to notice Blake.

He didn't give a damn about them. All he wanted was to find Mick. And to do that, he would have to check out the bedrooms. From the looks of the small, 1950's ranch house, he guessed that a pair of bedrooms faced the rear of the house.

Backtracking, he moved to the side yard and eased open its cedar gate. Luck was with him. One of the bedroom windows was open, its curtains gently stirring in the soft night breeze. He removed the screen, pushed aside the curtain, and climbed in. Two unmade twin beds, but no Mick.

His heartbeat pulsing, his gun drawn, he moved stealthily down a short, dark, carpeted hall toward the back of the house, paying close attention to the intonations coming from the front room. Any lessening of the excitement, any lull in the noise and he was flying back out that window.

Two more small bedrooms and a retro-tiled, postage-stamp sized bathroom gave onto the hallway. Luck was still with him. The doors were open.

More beds with rumpled sheets. But no Mick.

Disappointment surged through him.

As he crept back to the room with the open window, he hoped to God none of the guys had to use the restroom. His luck held again. A moment later, he was scurrying from the house.

But then his luck failed. He had not reckoned on the dog which began to bark viciously. As soon as Blake's boots touched the grass, the pit bull came charging. Adrenalin pumping in his veins, Blake raced toward the gate, but the dog lunged at him, nearly knocking him off his feet. As he steadied himself, the beast clamped its teeth into Blake's lower leg, as Blake shimmied the leg in an effort to dislodge the dog's deathly grip.

As much as he did not like boot-to-mouth combat with the four-legged menace, he hated more the prospect of a close-range encounter with Skinhead and the Glock. He had to get the hell out of here before they investigated the dog's unrelenting growls. Blake pummeled the beast with his good leg, the last, scooping swipe with the toe of his

boots launching the animal into the air —
with a chunk of Blake's jeans still in its
mouth.

Two sweeping steps brought Blake to the
gate. He just barely managed to slam it
against the bulldog's fresh assault.

Then he ran like hell.

But not before the front door of the house
banged open, and some choice Spanish cuss
words were hurled at him.

They had seen him. Chances were, they
recognized him, too, from the parking garage.

He sprinted as fast as his legs would carry
him back to the truck. They followed. At least
two of them. Possibly more.

Reaching into his pocket for the key lock
slowed him down, but still he jumped into his
pickup a good fifteen yards ahead of his
pursuers. He shoved in the key, slammed the
pickup into gear, and peeled out of there, the
accelerator pressed to the floorboard.

Because they had chosen to follow on foot
instead of car — or Hummer — he knew they
wouldn't be able to catch up with him by the
time they did get back to their vehicle. But if
they had a brain in their head, they would
not only have a description of his truck but
also the plate numbers. *Damn!*

"I'm not going to say `I told you so'," Ava
croaked from her squatted position on the
truck's floor.

"Then don't." He had to be going at least

seventy, through residential streets, no less.

Within minutes, he was back on a divided highway and doing eighty. He still needed to get some distance between him and the Hummer which would almost certainly be trying to find him.

* * *

Estrada picked up his phone. "Why in the hell you calling me at one in the morning?"

"Because that guy from the parking garage this morning just showed up at our house."

Estrada cursed. "You sure it's the same one?"

"I'm sure."

"You kill him?"

"No, he got away, but we're trying to follow him. He got a head start. We may need some help."

"What kind of car's he driving?"

"A white pickup. Late model. Texas license plates. CVG 492."

"I'll have my friends at the PD run the plates and see what we can come up with on the guy. You got a description of him?"

"Anglo. Dark hair. Tall. Maybe six two or three. Probably weighs two fifteen. Around thirty years old."

"Keep looking for him. All night if you have to. And kill the bastard." As an afterthought, he asked, "Was the *chica* with him?"

"No. He was alone."

* * *

The ibuprofen wasn't working. Now the chills had returned. She could not remember when she had ever felt so horrible. It was like the flu times two. And she really, really wanted to climb into a nice, soft bed.

But she could not tell Blake.

Her teeth chattering like castanets, she hugged her arms against the bone-deep chills. She hated her own weakness, hated that the tears began to roll down her cheeks. She felt so awful.

"Are you all right?" he asked.

She shrugged. "Just upset." She couldn't let him know about her physical limitations. Let him blame her behavior on mental strain.

"I'm taking you back to the house," he said. "You've had a rough day. You need a good night's sleep.

"I'm fine."

"You're saying that because you think I need you, but I don't. In fact, I can manage better when I don't have to worry about your safety."

She pictured the kindly doctor at Breckenridge Hospital and could almost hear his warning about rushing back to the hospital were she to run a fever. Good lord, she wondered, so hot and dizzy and miserable, am I going to die?

Maybe she should go back to their safe house, then take a cab — without Blake knowing about it — to the hospital while

Blake continued to look for Mick.

"All right," she finally said.

His voice lowered with concern. "You're not running a fever, are you?"

He didn't need to waste time taking her to the hospital — which is what he would insist upon. "No."

"Good. Sleep will be the best thing for you."

He headed toward the freeway, continuing to watch his rear-view mirror to make certain no one was following. They would be at the house in no more than ten minutes. In her present state, it was a strangely comforting thought.

She grew more mellow as they sped through the dark night. Blake, her dear Blake, had sensed her discomfort. No one had ever been able to read her like he did. It seemed almost unfathomable that she had only reunited with him less than forty-eight hours previously. In so many ways it seemed as if they had never parted. In so many ways they had seemed to pick up where they left off so many years ago. The smallest little details they'd once shared with each other came rushing back as clearly as this morning's headlines.

By his skeptical response when she told him she loved him, she knew he would be reluctant to ever trust her again. So reluctant that he'd fight his own softening emotions toward her, but she was prepared to fight to win him back.

After they found their son.

* * *

The location of his and Ava's safe house was as unknown as the origins of Stonehenge. No one else — not even Pete — knew of its existence. At no point that day or night had Blake been followed. Of that he was sure. His certainty in the secrecy of the bungalow should have allayed his fears for Ava's safety.

But it didn't.

The very idea of just dropping her off there made his blood run cold. His first instinct was to have one of his field guys guard her. But the need to find Mick demanded every person in Lone Star Investigations. None could be spared merely to ease his unfounded worry.

As he and Ava sped toward central Austin on the unusually empty freeway, she was unusually quiet. Which made him uneasy as hell. She had to be in pretty bad shape to have thrown in the towel on the search for their son.

He was seized with remorse that he had not insisted she rest, seized with guilt that he might have aggravated her wound by making love with her. But despite his self-loathing, he knew he would have been incapable of refusing her.

A man could live a lifetime and never experience more shatteringly fulfilling lovemaking than Ava had given him that night. At the memory, his breath shortened to hurried gasps.

Despite the nine years that had passed, despite the acrimony of their parting, despite that she had deprived him of his son, he still loved Ava Simpson. He realized now that he'd probably never stopped loving her.

He realized, too, there was a master plan for everyone's life. Baseball had been excluded from his master plan. But Ava could never be.

He could not plan anything beyond tonight — beyond finding Mick. But he kept recalling her words. *I love you.* He wanted to believe her. If he were honest with himself, spending his life with Ava was all he'd ever wanted. When this crisis was over would he be able to put behind them all the pain she had caused and march forward into a new life with her?

Would she be agreeable?

In so many ways she was the same Ava he had fallen in love with when they were teenagers, but in others she was vastly different.

For nearly a decade he had been convinced Ava did not possess maternal instinct. Now he knew better. Maybe it was the hormonal changes that occurred as a result of carrying a child to term, for now Ava exuded motherly tenderness. In spades.

He even believed that tenderness — that love — extended to him.

He hoped to God he was not misjudging her.

"You can just drop me off at the house," she said as they approached the sleeping neighborhood where the house was located.

"No can do."

"But you've got to continue searching- - -"

"For the kid," he said with a nod. "I know. Quit worrying. I'll keep looking. *After* I make sure the house is secure."

"I can't help worrying."

Nor could he. He worried like hell about her and the boy.

He circled the block once before pulling into the driveway, making certain there were no suspicious vehicles in the neighborhood.

Shoving the pickup into Park, he turned to her. "You stay here — with the doors locked — while I check out the house."

A nod was her only response. He did not like her quietness.

Hand on gun, he went through the tiny house, turning on lights and checking closets and beneath beds.

Assured that no one knew of the house, he went back to the truck, opened the passenger-side door, and gently lifted her wispy body into his arms. To his surprise, she did not protest.

After entering the house, he carried her straight to the bed, laid her on it, then retraced his steps and locked the front door.

Back in the bedroom, he helped her get beneath the crisp new sheets, then he fished her cell phone from her purse and laid it on her pillow. "Call 9-1-1, then me if anything's suspicious. Or if you think you've got fever." He quickly programmed his cell number into her speed dial. "I've put my number on the Eight button for quick calling."

She braided her fingers through his, nodded, then let her hand fall back into the bed.

He didn't like the lethargic look in her eyes, didn't like the heat he'd felt in her hand. "You sure you're not running fever?"

Her eyes looked unbelievably sorrowful as she nodded.

Hell, she's the nurse. She ought to know more about fevers than he.

"Need more ibuprofen?" he asked in a gentle voice, leaning toward the scoop of her body and wanting like hell to kiss her.

She shook her head. "Go on."

Before he left, he made sure every window was locked and each outside door secured with deadbolts.

Walking away from her was the hardest thing he had ever done.

But he had to. For the boy.

Logic told him no one could possibly find

her. Yet, with the same certainty he knew he was destined to carry his love for Ava to the grave, he feared he could not keep her safe.

Chapter 10

He felt like a flimsy lifeboat battered by angry waves. He was no longer bull's-eye certain he could save those desperate to survive, those who kept piling in. How much more could he take on before they would all sink to the bottom of the sea?

To lose Ava was incomprehensible. To lose the son he could never acknowledge, the son who resembled him in so many ways, was just as intolerable.

But as he drove through the dark streets of an unfamiliar city, he fought against the conviction that he could not save either of them. Dammit, he had to save them!

His cell phone rang. His heartbeat skidded, and his breath trapped in his pounding chest. Had something happened to Ava?

With the same compulsion to scan lists of disaster fatalities while terrified of discovering a loved one's name, he waited a moment — his stomach lurching — before answering in a shaky voice. "Tranowski." Blazing fear hammered into every pore of his body.

"I'm in Austin," Pete said. "Wanna meet?"

Relief flooded Blake. "Wish I could, but I can't lose a single minute."

"What can I do to help?"

Thank God Pete wasn't pushing for complete disclosure. "Between now and daylight we need to split up and search as many properties as we can, looking for the little boy who I believe is being held by Pacheco's gang."

"And what properties would this be?"

"All the ones in Travis County owned by Pacheco or his half brother." Blake swerved his pickup into the parking lot of a closed convenience store and turned off the ignition. "I'll send the list of addresses to your phone, then we can decide how to divvy it up."

He proceeded to transfer the data to his partner's smartphone. Once Pete had the list on his phone's screen, Blake asked, "How familiar are you with Austin?"

"Not very."

"I was hoping you'd have more knowledge of the city than I." He took a deep breath, tried to expel haunting thoughts of Ava, then continued. "Why don't we divide up the list by zip codes?"

"That's as good a way as any."

"I'll try to hit those in Austin proper, those with seven-eight-seven zips."

"Then I'll take those in the neighboring bedroom communities, like West Lake Hills and Del Valle." Pete paused. "You got a description of the kid?"

"Eight years old. Dark hair and eyes. Answers to the name Mick." Blake's tone turned deadly serious. "Most important of all, Pete, he could be in serious danger."

"And you know this because?"

"He may have witnessed his mother's murder. We found her body at that warehouse I asked you to have the boys watch. We also found the kid's Game Boy there."

"You can't go up alone against these thugs! Surely you've called the police."

"Not yet."

"Because you think Pacheco's got cops on his payroll?"

"I can't risk the boy."

Pete did not say anything for a minute. "So who was with you when you found the woman's body?"

"The female who was shot earlier."

"A client?"

"No. Just an old friend."

"An old friend you'd jeopardize your life for?"

Pete's mama didn't raise any dummies. "I guess so."

"What's she to the kid?"

Blake hesitated a minute before answering. "His mother."

"But I thought you said you and this chick

found his mother dead."

Blake sighed. "The boy has two mothers. . . and two fathers. I'm one of them."

* * *

Beneath the thick, black mustache, Estrada's lip curled into a smile when his cell phone rang. It would be Macinvale. In less than half an hour the homicide detective would have learned everything Estrada needed to know about the guy in the white pickup.

Macinvale always delivered. He was worth every penny of the five grand they wired into his wife's account the first of every month.

"What ya got?" Estrada snapped into the phone.

"Name's Blake Tranowski. Age twenty-nine. Resides in San Antonio. And, get this, the guy owns a private detective agency: Lone Star Investigations."

"What in the hell's a private dick doing snoopin' around my boys?"

"It may have something to do with your boys shooting at him."

"How'd you know about that?"

"Tranowski's name was in an Austin PD report this morning — or should I say yesterday morning — after a shooting that took place at the Town Lake Plaza Hotel parking garage. From the description of the perps, I figured the shooters were you and Pacheco's boys. The report was filed at

Breckenridge Hospital."

"Was this Tranowski hit?"

"No. That would be his female companion, one Ava Simpson. Age twenty-seven."

The same bitch who'd been nosing around Meecham's office. Bad break that she survived the attack he had ordered. Had she gone and hired a P.I.? Or could that son of a bitch Meecham have hired one?

"Any way you can have police find this Tranowski and take him into custody tonight?"

Macinvale did not respond for a moment. "If I have to trump up a false report against him, I could jeopardize myself. . ."

"How much?"

"I could lose my job, maybe even my pension. And I might face criminal charges and have to hire a high-priced lawyer- - -"

"How much?" Estrada snapped.

"At least fifty thousand."

"I'll wire it tonight."

Like the sizzling August heat in a Texas border town, rage pounded into him. He'd now be out fifty thousand stinking dollars because Manny Gonzales couldn't put a bullet into a broad's head.

As angry as he was with Manny, he was even madder at that damn Meecham. He punched Meecham's number into his phone.

* * *

Once Blake had seen her slip into the bed

and bolted the door behind himself, she reached for her cell phone. The festering shoulder throbbed in protest when she punched in the numbers, first, for information, then to call the taxi.

Every muscle in her body screamed with pain as she waited for the cab to arrive. If Blake should came back and find her gone, he would panic. She had to leave him a note. When she moved her hand to compose the note, blinding pain assaulted her, but with tears pricking her eyes, she forced herself to write to explain her whereabouts.

Fifteen minutes later, she was at the emergency room at Breckenridge Hospital explaining the symptoms that had compelled her to return.

"I'll just put you in an examination room, Miss Simpson," the attending nurse said. "I'm sure they'll want to get you started on IVs as soon as possible."

Before they went to the examination room, the nurse retrieved Ava's records from earlier in the day, attached them to a clipboard, and led the way to a tiny room. "I don't suppose your contact info has changed since this morning, has it?"

"No." Ava's teeth chattered.

"Just set your purse on a chair and hop up on the table."

Ava lay on the cold examination table and with her voice cracking as if she were about to cry, asked, "Could you please bring me a blanket?"

The nurse smiled down at her, stroking her forehead. "My, but you *do* have a fever! I'll bring you a nice, hot blanket."

The room was cold. Which explained why the nurse had worn a white cardigan. Even if fever hadn't been ravaging Ava's body, she would have found the room as cold as a meat locker.

The nurse promptly returned with the promised blanket and placed it over Ava's shivering body, tucking it beneath her. "Now let me take your temp. Since your teeth are chattering so, I'll just slip the thermometer into your armpit."

When she saw the bandage around Ava's left armpit, she moved to the right. "We don't want to disturb your wound any more than necessary.

"No wonder you're so miserable," the nurse exclaimed a moment later when she saw the thermometer's digital readout. "A hundred and three!"

She recorded the temperature, then retucked the blanket around Ava. "The doctor will be in a moment. Hopefully."

Ava lay shivering in the brightly lit, sterile room, so tired and aching, she prayed for sleep.

She was drifting into slumber when the door opened. All she saw was a man in a white lab coat moving toward her. He came and pulled away the blanket.

Only when he reached to inject her with a syringe did she see his white sleeve lift to reveal a tattoo.

The last thing she remembered was gasping as she looked up at his shaved head.

Chapter 11

The lurch of the vehicle as it chugged uphill through the inky darkness awakened her. That, and the swirling contents of her stomach. The prattle of youthful male voices speaking Spanish in the front seat jarred her memory. . .

One of Pacheco's gang must have taken her from the hospital after injecting her with that syringe.

She had no desire for her captors to know she had awakened. Without opening her eyes, she could tell there were two guys in the front and another beside her. What she couldn't figure out was why hadn't they already killed her.

Why hadn't they just injected her with a lethal drug? There had to be a reason for keeping her alive. She suspected she was in for some brutal questioning. They'd want to know why she was seeking Mick. They'd have to find out who she was working with.

Then they would kill her.

She had to get away from these lowlifes before they killed her, but how? There was no one to help her. She had thoroughly excluded the one person who could have protected her.

Bitter regret surged through her. She had once again withheld the truth from Blake. And once again it would cost her dearly. This time it would cost her life.

If only she could call Blake's cell. A flutter of hope lifted her dragging spirits. Her captors might have brought along her purse. If only she could get her hands on the phone. If only she could call Blake.

Still pretending to be asleep, she felt first to her left, then to her right, for her big leather bag. Nothing. As immovable as a dead person, she barely cracked open one eye. It took a moment before her narrow line of vision adjusted to the dark. She scanned the floorboard of the back seat of what she suspected was a Hummer. Nothing.

So much for getting her hands on her cell phone.

She wasn't sure if it were the residual effects of the drug or her paralyzing fear that escalated her nausea. The higher the SUV climbed, the sicker she became. Physical discomfort definitely took a backseat to the horrifying prospect of being killed. She had not thought about the fever or the throbbing pain in her shoulder, though she had been dazedly conscious of the raging heat that threatened to consume her, of the achiness that penetrated into every muscle of her body.

But she could not dwell on that — not when her very life was at stake. She had to get away from these murderers. But how could anyone as sick and weak as she outmaneuver the healthy young males who had abducted her?

Even if she succeeded in playing for the element of surprise when they reached their destination, she would hardly be able to outrun her captors.

A deep, retching hopelessness weakened her as effectively as the nausea rising in her queasy belly.

The wisest course might be to continue acting unconscious. Perhaps she would then be able to overhear what their plans for her were. It would be much easier to prepare a sound defense if she knew the offense.

Instinct, though, told her that her chances of survival were better outdoors than in, especially if they were going — as she suspected — to a remote location. Once they had her within four walls, her avenues for escape would be shut off.

And she did have darkness on her side, the kind of deep darkness which only occurs when the lights of a city and its environs are far away.

Even though she was sicker than she'd ever been in her life, she had no choice but to make her break when the thugs went to lift her limp and lifeless body from the car's backseat. She would rather risk a bullet in the back than face a gory death like that which had claimed Elaine Meecham. Damn that Walter Meecham!

They turned off the main road. The choppy ride made her feel as if she were going to upchuck at any second. They must be on a dirt road.

Then they turned again, and the guy riding shotgun got out and slammed his door shut. From just outside the vehicle she heard the squeaking noise of what must be a gate opening. That he had not left his door open told her they must be mere feet away from their destination.

Her pulse thundered.

In a matter of seconds she would try to escape.

Or would she?

The utterance of a single word — one of the few Spanish words she knew — changed her course of action: *Nino.* A little boy. He must still be alive!

They must have brought her to where Mick was being held! No way was she leaving this property without the child.

Even if they killed her.

Instead of continuing to pretend to still be unconscious, she sat up. In those first few seconds she scanned the back seat, making sure her purse — and a possible link to Blake — was not there.

Even though she had known it wouldn't be there, disappointment coursed through her pain-wracked body when she confirmed that none of her possessions had been brought.

The guy beside her whirled to face her while saying something in Spanish to his companion in the front seat.

Then he pulled a gun.

At first she thought he was going to kill her right there, now that they were away from witnesses. Then she realized he was merely using the gun to deter her from trying to escape.

The driver came to a stop, got out of the vehicle, then walked around to her side and opened the door.

Gagging, she lunged toward the open space and proceeded to throw up.

Give the guy credit. He had the decency to back away and offer her a moment of privacy. Or maybe he'd just wimped out. She would have tried to capitalize on that moment of privacy if it weren't for her need to get to Mick.

Despite the sickness, she tried to take stock of her surroundings. A single-story house was less than twenty feet away, and towering pines swept around its perimeter. No other houses could be seen, but she thought she heard the lapping of water. Could they be by a lake?

When she finished retching, she was able

to see a sliver of white behind the house and realized it was a boat. That was when she remembered Pacheco had a property up at Lake Travis. That must be where they were.

If only she could get to a phone, but that possibility was as unobtainable as the man she would have called. The only man she had ever loved.

One thing seemed certain: Meecham and Estrada needed to find out how much she knew and who she had talked to before they extinguished her life.

But they couldn't get information out of someone who was unconscious. . .

She stepped away from the car, then as naturally as blinking an eye, she collapsed onto the dirt drive. Gravel bit into her sensitive flesh and embedded itself in her cheek.

Her captors spouted a bevy of Spanish cuss words, felt for a pulse, then lifted her to carry her into the house.

They reverently addressed an older man in the first room they entered. It must be Estrada. More Spanish was spoken. Then, fortunately, English: "Put her in the room with the kid."

With Mick! Her glee at the prospect of seeing the boy almost compensated for the waves of incredible sickness that zapped her like a flyswatter knocking down insects.

The guy carrying her walked another ten

yards then stopped, and she heard metal slide into metal. A key in a door lock. Then a door opened.

And her heart broke. The child — the child whose cries had seared into her sleep for so many nights — was weeping.

Now that she had finally found the boy, she was powerless to help him.

The guy tossed her onto a bed as if she were a bale of hay. The pain to her shoulder was so intense she almost cried out, but she managed to continue acting unconscious while he strode back to the door and locked it.

Once she was alone with Mick behind the locked bedroom door, she opened her eyes. The room was totally dark. The windows must have been boarded over. Her nausea gone now, she rose. "Does the dark frighten you?" she whispered.

"I don't know."

At the very sound of his voice, an overwhelming sense of love crashed over her. His husky voice sounded different — less babyish and more rugged — than it had in her dreams. And its tone distinctly resembled Blake's.

She walked toward where she thought the door was and felt for a light switch. She flipped it, but did not immediately turn around to face Mick. First, she had to pull herself together. She couldn't start bawling at the sight of his tear-streaked face. She couldn't rush to him and smother him with kisses. She couldn't let him know she was the woman who had given him birth.

Nervous and fluttery and excited all at the same time, she finally allowed herself to face the child she had not seen since the day of his birth.

No matter how well she had schooled herself to be stoic, she could not look upon his adorableness without watery eyes. The same sense of wondrous awe that had consumed her when she saw his photo struck her ten times more powerfully now.

A little hunk. A precious little hunk. Even with eyes red from crying, he was the best looking, most masculine looking little boy she had ever seen. So very much like Blake. Adored Blake.

She could compose a check list of Blake's physical attributes, and Mick would possess every one. Healthy olive complexion. Check. Hair the color of strong coffee. Check. Black eyes. Check. Narrow waist paired with lengthy, powerful legs. Check.

He wore scruffy baseball pants. With a Yankees t-shirt. Which tore her up.

How could she ever have deprived Blake of the boy who was his son in every way? She deserved to have lost his love. She had most certainly forfeited her right to be this child's mother. She even deserved to die from the complications of her gunshot wound.

The poor little guy looked scared. "Are you afraid of those bad men, too?" he asked.

She was not sure how to answer. More than anything, she wished to offer him security. "I am, but if there's any way to get you away from them, I will try."

He started crying again. "I want my mother. Is she really dead? Those bad men told me she was."

Thank God he hadn't witnessed his mother's brutal murder.

She did not want to lie. She did not want to give him false hope, either. But he could not learn the painful truth at this time. He had already been through far too much.

She stepped toward his bed and sat beside him. "All I can tell you, dearest Mick, is that since your mother could not be here, she wanted me to come and take care of you."

"You won't let those bad men hurt me?"

"They'd have to kill me first."

He batted away the evidence of his crying. "How come you know me?"

"Because I'm. . .friends with you mother."

"Do you have any children?"

She hesitated a moment. "No."

"Do you know my father?"

For a second, she thought he was talking about Blake. At that very instant she had been wishing Blake would find them, that he would bring the police to deal with the criminals who were holding them. "I've met him, but I don't really know him."

"I wish Daddy would come. He said he would come get me on Friday. What day is it?"

"Wednesday," she answered. "No, make that Thursday morning. You've talked to your father since . . .you left home?"

"Every night they let me talk to him."

That horrible, horrible man! Putting his poor child through all this. Cavorting with known criminals. Having his wife murdered. He was the one who should be lying in that warehouse with his throat slashed.

Mick turned away, smashed his face into the pillow, and wept.

Using the last bit of her waning strength, her hands swept gentle circles over his heaving little back. "Honey, I know it's been awful for you."

"I want my mother," he whimpered.

This was even worse than those terrifying dreams. At least then she believed she could help him if only she could find him.

Now she had found him, and there was nothing she could do to bring him solace.

"I know, love. I know." She stroked his dark, damp hair. It curled at the nape of his neck.

Just like Blake's.

Having soaked in every detail the child's appearance, she now allowed herself to survey the tiny room that was their prison. Its only furnishings were a pair of old metal-framed twin beds equipped with cheap mattresses without any bedding. There was neither a bedside table nor a lamp, nor a chest of drawers.

She got up to inspect the window. It had been boarded on the outside. She tried to raise the lower portion of the double-hung glass, but the wood frame had been hammered against the sash.

Next she tried the door, even though she had heard the distinct sound of it being locked. No go there, either.

If escape was impossible, she would settle for the opportunity to make a clandestine phone call. One quick, quiet call to Blake, and she knew his competence would take over. He would get them out of there.

There were bound to be extension phones in the other bedrooms, but how could she get to one? She lifted her head toward the rectangular air conditioning vent. Its opening wasn't any larger than a piece of notebook paper. And even if it could be enlarged, how in the heck could she climb up and hoist her body into the hole?

There must be a way. . . But for now she must lie down. She was too weak to continue standing. She must lie down beside her baby.

* * *

Blake had finally figured a way around

Austin's monstrous traffic problem. Make sure to drive mid week — and only after two in the morning. His truck breezed down North Lamar with hardly another vehicle in sight.

According to his GPS, Estrada's place on Shoal Creek was only another mile away. He hoped to God Mick would be there.

And he hoped to God Ava was OK. Every instinct he possessed told him she was in danger. He must have spent too much time with her. He was beginning to think like her. Ava and her silly instincts. . .Only her instincts had proven to lead them to a clear and present danger.

He'd fought against the urge to call her. For cryin' out loud, he'd taken her home so she could get some badly needed sleep. He didn't need to go and awaken her only to allay his own unfounded fears.

And now he had one more fear. The same pair of headlights had been behind him now for the past several blocks. Estrada's men?

There was only one way to find out. He swerved a quick right at the next corner and put pedal to the metal to get the hell out of there.

The car followed.

Blake clipped around the next corner.

Lights flashed. Police lights.

He'd done nothing that would warrant being pulled over by the police. He'd been especially careful not to go over the speed limit. He'd used his turn signal. His truck was new, with all its lights in good working order.

It could be a trick. It could be Estrada's thugs. Or. . . it could be the Austin PD Blake knew how easy it would be for someone like Estrada to grease the right palms to get out an A.P.B. for the white truck ID'd by the Hummer slime balls.

This was his confirmation that Estrada and his murdering brother really did have someone in the police department on their payroll.

Chapter 12

His first instinct was to try to outrace the cop. But he'd been a cop. He knew the impossible odds. The cops always won.

So he pulled over to the side of the residential street, right under the bright glow of a street light. He had a few seconds lead time after he brought the vehicle to a stop while the officer radioed in his whereabouts.

The cop would have already run a check on Blake's plates. He might even have been told that Blake was armed and dangerous. Blake's immediate priority was to win the policeman's trust.

Then he could disarm him.

Blake threw open his truck's door, and with hands raised far above his head, he exited the vehicle and kicked the door shut. He knew how scared and vulnerable a lone policeman could be in the wee hours of the morning. He'd lived that life. "I don't know why you're stopping me, officer. I didn't break any traffic laws."

The cop looked like a rookie. A skinny kid who was a good four or five inches shorter than Blake. Frail and fair and not able to fill out his uniform. Weapon drawn, he strode toward Blake. "May I see your identification?"

"Sure. I know the drill. I'm former San Antonio PD" One arm still high above his head, Blake reached into his back pocket with the other hand.

"Is that so?" The young officer cracked a sliver of a smile as he circled Blake to make sure there wasn't a gun in that back pocket.

Blake withdrew the billfold, then used both hands to retrieve his driver's license. He held it close to his body when he offered it to the cop.

As the young patrolman reached for it, Blake's knee rammed him in the groin. The cop doubled over. With a lightning swift move, Blake grabbed the gun before the officer could control his automatic reflex.

Aiming the pistol at the cop, he ordered him back to the squad car. With one hand, Blake grabbed the handcuffs and affixed one to the steering wheel. "I'm really sorry, brother," Blake said as he cuffed the young officer. "Was there an arrest warrant for whoever was driving my pickup?"

The patrolman nodded.

"If you want to be a hero, find out who ordered it. Then you'll have the rotten cop who's on the take. That guy's owned by Carlos Pacheco."

The policeman's eyes rounded.

Blake started to walk away, then spun back around. "Just so that you'll know. . . Until five minutes ago, I was on the right side of the law, buddy."

* * *

He could take the back roads through residential neighborhoods to reach Pacheco's place on Shoal Creek. For now, police would be racing down North Lamar to where a fallen officer had been reported. They would not be combing the residential streets. Yet.

In another ten minutes they would.

He punched in Pete's number. "Got a problem."

"What's that?"

Blake quickly filled him in. "I'm gonna ditch the truck here and walk to the property Pacheco owns on Shoal Creek. It's less than a mile way. On the other side of North Lamar from here. Since I'll need a fresh vehicle, I need you to meet me there."

"What's the address?"

"Sixty-two, fifteen Shoal Creek."

"Ten-four. And, Blake?"

"Yeah?"

"Be careful. Especially crossing North Lamar. The place is bound to be crawling with cops now."

* * *

He might have to rethink this business of wearing nothing but white shirts. Here in a sleeping neighborhood, he would not arouse suspicion, but once he reached the boulevard, he could be seen from blocks away. Like Pete said, the place would now be crawling with cops.

If he could be assured the backup would be coming from central Austin, he would be OK going north of his present location before crossing the major thoroughfare.

But when a cop was down, the fallen colleague's fellow law enforcement officers would converge on the scene from all points throughout the city.

One thing was for sure. Blake needed to get as far away from his pickup — and the cuffed cop — as fast as he could. He began to sprint toward North Lamar, taking note of every bush that could hide him if a car turned onto the street.

He made it to the major street without seeing another moving vehicle, but as he approached the intersection, a siren blared. A police car sped toward him.

He dove behind a pickup that was parked on the corner's used car dealership. The squad car rounded the corner not more than fifteen feet from him. His pulse thundered.

When the car proceeded toward the location of the downed cop, Blake swished a sigh of relief.

He would have to act quickly to cross the street before more screaming emergency vehicles converged on the same intersection.

He bolted from behind the row of vehicles and darted onto North Lamar. He quickly crossed the street before he heard the second siren, this one coming from the north.

Seconds later, Blake was safely jogging along Shoal Creek, looking for sixty-two, fifteen. With its broad, well-kept front yards and sleepy, sprawling ranch houses, this neighborhood looked like the kind of place where he would like to raise a family, the kind of place he would like to share with Ava. And their kids.

But the only kid he wanted was Mick, who already had a father. Blake should hate Ava from depriving him of Mick. He was still angry as hell at her, but hatred was one emotion she would never elicit in him. Not when every beat of his heart resonated with love for her.

He loved Mick, too, even though he'd never had the pleasure of seeing him in the flesh. His chest tightened at the thought of this kid who meant so much to him. He had to find him, had to rescue him from Pacheco's gang.

Another block, and he'd be at the property. A car turned onto the street. His heart pounded. He scanned his surroundings. No bushes, but he thought he might could hide that damned white shirt behind the thick trunk of the mature oak tree three strides away. He ducked behind the tree as the slowly moving car approached this block.

When it pulled abreast of him, Blake saw

it was Pete's sports car. He sprang from behind the tree and began to wave.

Pete saw him, stopped, and lowered the window. "Get in, bud."

Blake climbed in the passenger side.

"You really have gotten yourself into some deep doo doo," Pete said, continuing down the street at twenty miles per hour.

"I don't care what happens to me. All that matters is finding that little boy."

Pete nodded. "What's that address? There at the white brick house."

"Wrong side of the street, pod-nah."

"So it is."

"Besides, that house looks too. . ."

"Too respectable for the likes of Carlos Pacheco?"

"Yeah."

"Well, bud, so does this."

Blake read the next address. Right place, but wrong look. "A VW Bug?"

"Not exactly what you'd expect from those murdering bastards, is it?"

"It's gotta be a rent house."

"I suspect someone with a bankroll like Pacheco's has a lot of rental property."

Like the paint and body shop he and Ava had seen earlier. "And cops he's making rich."

"You think that's why you were pulled over? Because a bad cop ordered it to appease Estrada?"

"I do." Blake gripped the door handle.

"Stop. I'm going to check out the place."

"The kid's not going to be there."

"I know. It's too nice a neighborhood, too close to law-abiding citizens. But I've got to make certain."

Pete hit the brakes and shoved the floor shift into Park. "I'll come with you."

"No. I want you to stay here. Be a lookout — and be ready for a quick getaway."

Blake padded through the well-clipped grass of the neighboring yard, scoping out the house in question. No lights. Which was to be expected at three-forty in the morning. He almost wished there were lights so he could take a look at the house's inhabitants.

He moved toward the backyard. No fence there — and hopefully no barking dogs. He closed in on the house, heading toward its rear. There was a simple little swing set. Almost new. He was almost positive this couldn't be the place where Mick would be held.

Looking at the swing set upset him almost as much as looking upon the murdered body of Mick's adoptive mother. It hurt to think Mick was being deprived of childhood activities or playing for his Little League team or breathing fresh air.

The bedrooms would be at the back of the house. The first one he came to was free of curtains. He pressed his face to the glass, but it was too dark to see anything inside. Then he shone his flashlight into the room. It was not a bedroom but a home office.

He tried the window, but it was locked. A tool attached to his Swiss Army knife easily cut through the glass, allowing him to unclasp the window's lock.

After raising the window, he climbed into the room. Gun drawn, he crept down the carpeted hallway, past a bathroom with its door open. Two more doors opened onto the hall, one with an open door, the other closed. He came to the one with the open door first, stood at the threshold, and turned on his flashlight.

The room was done totally in hot pink. A little girl's room. The tiny little blonde slept on a tiny little bed in the corner.

He need not go any further. This wasn't the place where he would find Mick. As quietly as he could, he left the same way he had entered.

Back in Pete's Porsche, he shook his head. "Don't say it."

"What? I told you so?"

Blake filled him in on what he'd discovered.

"Good work."

But there was nothing good about the way Blake felt. He was once again back to Square One. No closer to finding Mick.

And he was still racked with worry about Ava.

His cell phone rang. His heartbeat accelerated as his hand flew to the phone. "Tranowski."

"Mr. Tranowski, I'm calling from Breckenridge Hospital."

Ava! Something had happened to Ava. "Is Ava all right?"

"I was hoping she was with you."

Fear sliced through him. "What do you mean?"

"She came here a couple of hours ago burning up with fever from the gunshot wound we had treated earlier in the day."

Why in the hell hadn't she told him? Dammit! She must have taken a taxi there. After lying to him. Again. "And. . .?"

"And she seems to have disappeared. We found her purse in the examination room."

Chapter 13

A hundred scenarios — all of them bad — raced through his mind. The simple explanation — and the most horrifying — was that Pacheco's henchmen had staked out the hospital. They had to have known Ava was shot, and they might be expecting her to seek medical help.

"How long was she alone in the examination room?" he asked, barely able to suppress the fear that slammed through him like a freight train.

"I'll have to ask the duty nurse."

"I'll ask her myself. I'll be there in ten minutes."

As soon as he terminated the call, Pete asked, "Be where?"

"Breckenridge Hospital. Step on it."

Pete downshifted his high-powered sports car and sped off toward North Lamar. "What's happened?"

"I think Pacheco's gang abducted Ava."

"Ava? Not *your* Ava from back in the minor leagues?"

"Yeah." *My Ava.* God, if only she was. If

only. . . if only he could find her before they sliced her throat like they'd done to Elaine Meecham. So many emotions pulsed through him: fear, rage, desperation, and love. Love that could be lost forever. "She's the kid's mother."

"Was she at Breckenridge?"

"Apparently so, though it was news to me." His fury was so intense he could shake her senseless.

If she was still alive.

"She was treated there for a gunshot wound earlier in the day. They told her to come back if she had any signs of fever."

"Why didn't *you* take her back to the hospital?"

"I didn't know. She obviously didn't want me to know."

"Because she wanted you to keep looking for the kid?"

"Obviously." Dammit, Ava!

* * *

Pete dropped him off at the hospital's emergency entrance while he parked.

"I'm Ava Simpson's . . .fiancé, and I need to talk to the nurse who attended her."

A middle-aged woman wearing scrubs and a white cardigan stepped up from behind a counter. "That would be me. You must be Mr. Tranowski."

He nodded. "Tell me what you know."

"I got her in a room right away and took

her vitals. She was running a temperature of a hundred and three."

"I wish to God she'd have told me."

"She was very sick."

"If she left the hospital on her own, she would have taken her purse."

"As sick as she was, I don't see that as a possibility. She was weak and drowsy."

So what happened after you took her vitals?"

"I left her alone in the room. When the doctor showed up a few minutes later, she was gone, and so was the gurney."

She must have been wheeled out of there. As horrifying as the thought was, it could have been worse. They could have killed her on the gurney. For some reason, they wanted her alive. Which meant there might be time for him to rescue her.

He opened his wallet and withdrew his identification. "I'm a private investigator. Mind if I question your co-workers?"

"Go ahead, but I think I'd better go ahead and notify the police department."

Not what he wanted. "My friend on the Austin PD, Detective Alvarez, will be here any second."

Just then Pete walked up. "Detective Alvarez," Blake said, "I was just telling the nurse that I'd asked you and the Austin PD to help investigate Ava's disappearance."

Pete froze for a fraction of a second, then

recovered and flashed his disarming smile at the nurse. Women were always suckers for Pete.

Blake filled him in on what the nurse had told him.

"Tell me, Miss. . ." Pete read her name tag. "Ms. Turner, have you seen any unfamiliar medical personnel on this floor tonight?"

"No. . . no, wait! I did. There was a youngish man with a shaved head. Hispanic. He was wearing a lab coat, and I assumed he was new, probably from x-ray. Half the emergency patients need to be collected and taken to x-ray."

Pete and Blake exchanged *Eureka!* glances. "That description matches that of the man who shot Miss...Ava today," Pete said.

Her hand clasped her mouth as if to stifle a scream. "Oh my God! I feel so awful."

"It's not your fault, Ms. Turner," Pete said, smiling at her as he turned to leave. "You've been very helpful. We'll put the police force on this right away."

* * *

"Deep doo doo," Pete reiterated once they were back in the Porsche. "First you accost a cop, and now you've got me impersonating a police officer. We could lose our license. Hell, we could go to prison!"

"I don't care. All that matters is finding Ava. And the kid."

Blake's cell phone rang again. Could it be

Ava? No, damn it, she didn't have his cell number. It was in her purse which was still at the hospital. Could it be the hospital calling? Had they found Ava? Maybe she'd been in the restroom, possibly lost consciousness there. But why was the gurney gone? "Tranowski."

It was one of his investigators. "I've been watching that warehouse you ordered surveillance on, and I thought you'd be interested to know someone just showed up."

Ava? His breath stopped in mid chest. "Who?"

"The Meecham dude. In his Mercedes."

"Alone?"

"Yep."

"Make sure he doesn't leave. I'll be there in ten minutes." If he had to kill the son of a bitch, he was going to find out where Ava was.

If they hadn't already killed her.

* * *

She had turned out the light. The poor little fellow needed sleep. As did she. Climbing on his bed and lying next to him, she had drawn him close, happy that he did not protest, that he snuggled into the curve of her. She stroked his damp hair and murmured endearments. Soon his whimpering ceased, and he fell asleep.

She slept, too, but her sleep was fitful, her aching body trembling from the fever which had continued to climb. Her thoughts went from lucid to surreal. One minute she would be praying that they would be rescued, that Mick would never have to learn the details of his adopted mother's brutal death. The next, she would be surrounded by gargoyle-looking creatures that were trying to kill her and Mick while laughing heinously.

Some time during those wee hours of the morning, the men in the house had retired to the bedrooms. She heard the shuffle of a man's shoes in the room next to hers, then quiet.

Now she was suddenly awakened from a terrifying nightmare. She tried to reach into her mind to remember why the dream was so frightening, but she had immediately forgotten it.

For the present had intruded, and she was not so sick that she'd lost the ability to comprehend. The male voice in the next room spoke, though she was sure she had not heard anyone else enter. Could he be on the phone?

Then she distinctly heard an address. The address where Elaine Meecham had been murdered. "If you want a demonstration of what can happen to your little boy, go to that address," the man in the next room said. Then she heard what sounded like a phone receiver slamming into its cradle.

* * *

Because there was almost no traffic at that

hour, they reached the warehouse in less than ten minutes. Pete slammed his car a couple of inches from the Mercedes' rear bumper to block it from leaving.

"You stay here," Blake said. "Estrada could show up at any minute."

"Then what do I do?"

"Call my cell, then the police."

As Blake approached the building, he remembered that he had not locked it after he had cleaned up earlier. He tried the door. It was still unlocked.

His gun drawn, he eased open the door and stepped into the dark hallway. He fleetingly wondered if Meecham would be armed. He thought not. A rich guy like that hired flunkies to do his dirty work.

Like killing his rich wife.

Why in the hell was the guy here? Was he such a sadist that he wanted to gloat over his wife's gory death? He must be one sick bastard.

Walking softly to muffle the sound of his footsteps, Blake made his way down the dark hallway. The further he went, the more distinctly he heard a man groaning. What the hell? His guys had been watching the building. No one had come except Meecham, and he'd been alone. No one could have injured Meecham.

A wedge of light spilled into the hallway from the room at the end. The room where the two bodies had been stashed. He approached the room cautiously, his gun ready, his pulse spiking. He paused long enough to collect his thoughts. Even if Meecham drew a weapon on him, he would shoot only to disarm him, not to kill. He was fairly confident that the reflexes of a twenty-nine-year-old were superior to that of a man sixty-five. Meecham must live. He had to help Blake find Ava and Mick.

He would use the steel door as a shield when he surprised Meecham. Drawing a deep breath, he pushed at the door.

Meecham looked up, but he wasn't armed.

Stunned, Blake lowered the gun. Meecham was on his knees beside his wife. Weeping.

In that instant, Blake realized how wrongly he had misjudged the man.

"What's going on, man?" Blake asked, his voice low and sympathetic.

"Are you the bastard who killed my wife?"

"No. I have nothing to do with Pacheco and his brother."

"Then what are you doing here?"

"I've been trying to find your son." It hurt like hell to call Mick this man's son.

His eyes glassy from crying, Meecham stared at Blake for a full minute. Then, in an anguished voice, he said, "You're Mick's real father, aren't you?"

Chapter 14

Blake nodded solemnly.

"She said Mick looked just like his father." Walter Meecham buried his face into his hands and wept, his bent-over shoulders heaving with his racking sobs.

"Who said?"

Meecham lifted his wet face, peered at Blake, then spoke in halted, emotionally wrenching snippets. "The woman who came to my office claiming to be his birth mother. She was obviously talking about you. The resemblance is very strong."

"The sons of bitches have taken her now. They also took Mick from here. We found a child's Game Boy game in this room earlier tonight."

"I hope to God my boy didn't see. . ." Meecham sagged, staring at the awful evidence of the killers' knife.

A moment later, he gathered his composure. "They'll kill Mick, too, if I don't lie on the witness stand tomorrow."

"You're the witness who saw Pacheco execute Orlando Garza?"

Meecham nodded. "One night when I was working late." He drew in a shaky breath. "I heard a car pull up in the parking lot very late. They didn't know I was there. I was parked behind the building. I looked out the window just in time to see the whole thing."

"They'll never let Mick go, you know. He can identify them. They'll kill him and flee to Mexico as soon as Pacheco's exonerated."

The older man collapsed onto his wife, sobbing.

"We've got to find him. Tonight. Do you have any idea where they might be?"

Meecham shook his head.

"How did you know to come here?"

"Estrada called me about half an hour ago. Told me to come here and see what would happen to Mick if I don't do as they say."

"My hunch is if we find him, we find Mick. And Ava. Can you think of anything you heard during that call? Something like a train whistle? Anything that will help us locate him?"

Meecham bolted up, his expression sharp. "As a matter of fact, I did! He always calls from his cell phone, but his battery must have been too low, forcing him to use a land line. The caller ID listed the Lakeway phone exchange."

"I've got the address!" Blake darted for the door. "We've been searching the properties owned by Pacheco and Estrada all night."

Meecham leaped to his feet. "I'm coming with you!"

When they reached the front of the building, Blake said, "Pete's car won't hold three. We'll take your car. You know Austin better than either of us. You drive."

After they got into the Mercedes and were speeding down the highway, Blake filled Pete in on what he had learned back at the building.

When he finished, Meecham said, "You really care about Mick, don't you?"

Blake shrugged. "I didn't even know of his existence until Monday. It's the damnedest thing. Now I'd give my life to save the kid."

"I hope to God we can," Meecham said, his voice choking with emotion.

* * *

Estrada hadn't been able to sleep. Something kept gnawing at him. He lay in the dark, his bedroom next to the Meecham kid's. And the bitch. The lighted numerals on the clock changed with each slowly passing moment. Three. Three thirty. Now it was four in the morning. He hadn't slept, and he felt like crap. And something kept nagging at him, something he couldn't put a finger on.

Then suddenly he shot up like a jack-in-the-box. Son of a bitch! He'd gotten careless. He'd slipped up and called Meecham from the land line.

He hadn't slipped up so much, though,

that he couldn't right his wrong. Dressing quickly, he roused the four other men in the house. "We've got to get the hell out of here. Pronto!"

Manuel rubbed his eyes against the glare of the overhead light Estrada had turned on. "What time is it?"

"Time to leave, *amigo*. Get dressed. We're taking the kid to the place in Del Valle. After we kill the woman."

"But I thought you were going to have me use my persuasive skills on her first."

"No time for that. I'd just as soon do away with her. We'll make it look like an accident."

Manuel knew better than to argue for more sleep. All their dirty activities had to be conducted under the cover of darkness, and it would soon be daylight.

* * *

She never heard the door slam open or the light switch tripped. It was Mick's gasp that awakened her. Just as the warmth of his body was yanked away from her.

"What are you doing to him?" she demanded as she shot up like a bullet.

Two of the younger men were tearing through a hemp rope with a switchblade knife. "It's not your concern, *chica*," the older man — Estrada? — said. "You'll be kissing the angels by the time we reach Del Valle."

They were going to kill her, but all she could think of was rescuing Mick.

"I want my mother!"

"Shut up, brat. Your mother's dead, and you'll be dead, too, if you don't get the hell out of here right now."

One of the men began to bind Mick's slim wrists, but Mick began to kick him. All four of the younger men collapsed around the feisty boy.

Ava leaped from the bed and tried to pull them off. Estrada crashed a tattooed arm into her face, propelling her back to the bed. Blood gushed from her nose. As dazed as she was, all she could think of was her need to protect Mick. She lunged again at the lowlifes who were hurting her baby. *I promised Mick I wouldn't let anything happen to him.* Once again, Estrada struck her, but this time — a sadistic look on his face — his fist arrowed into her shoulder wound. She cried out in blinding pain.

And this time she fell to the floor. Something snapped in her back when she hit the ground.

She tried to rise again, but she could not even lift her head.

She lay on the floor, her eyes misting as she helplessly watched Estrada's men lift both of Mick's legs and twist the rope around his ankles. Once they had his hands and feet bound, one of them tore off a length of duct tape and strapped it over his mouth.

Tears glistened on his cheeks as he tossed

Ava an imploring look as if to say *I thought you said you wouldn't let them hurt me.*

"Lock him in the van," Estrada ordered, "then come back and help me with her."

They're going to kill me. And she couldn't even move, not even when her very life depended on it.

"I know who you are," she said, "and I'm not the only one. If anything happens to me or to Mick, you will pay with your life."

"And just who do you think I am?" the older man sneered.

"You're Julio Estrada, Carlos Pacheco's half brother."

"Too bad you won't live to tell anyone."

"I left a note for one of my associates. They're all looking for you as we speak."

A flicker of fear registered in his black eyes. "Who are these associates of yours?"

She had nothing to lose. No way would she jeopardize Blake. "San Antonio policemen. You'll never get away with it."

He said something in Spanish to one of the men who had stayed behind, and the other man took a switchblade from his pocket, eying her.

Her heart hammered. She was going to end up just like Elaine Meecham.

The man with knife slid his gaze to the rope and proceeded to slice off two more lengths of rope.

Why were they going to tie the rope around

her? Why not just slit her throat? "They *will* find you," she spit out. "If you don't hurt the boy, there may be some leniency."

An evil glint in his eye, Estrada moved toward her and planted a foot on either side of her trunk, then lowered himself on top her, straddling her. "Why are you shaking so, *chica*? Do I scare you?"

She wouldn't give him the satisfaction. "I'm not scared of a loser like you, a man who threatens innocent children. If I'm shaking, it's from the fever."

He removed a handkerchief from his pocket and wiped away the blood from her face. "It's a shame to torch a pretty little thing like you."

"Torch?" she rasped.

"It will look like an accident. The rope will burn up right along with you."

"My associates know I would never have come here of my own free will. They'll track you down."

"But didn't you say you and your associates were looking for me? That would easily explain how you came to be here. If only you hadn't gone poking that nose of yours into affairs that were none of your business." He clasped both her flailing arms, her strength no match for his.

The other man tightened the rope at her wrists so tightly that it cut into her flesh. Then he moved to her ankles while Estrada continued to straddle her. They had finished before the two others returned.

"Put her on the bed and tie her to the mattress," Estrada ordered.

She lay helpless on the bed as they pulled a single length of rope around her, running it under the bed and bringing it fully around her before tying it at her stomach. Just like a present. What a sick, sick present.

After Estrada said something in Spanish, one of the younger men wadded up paper into a metal trash can, placed it beside the window, and ignited it with a match.

In a moment or two the flame would reach the curtain. In ten minutes, she would probably be dead.

Estrada laughed as he cut off the light and left the room. "*Adios, chica.*"

Despair seeping into every pore of her body, she envied Elaine Meecham her quick death.

Chapter 15

It sickened Blake when he realized Estrada's location was not in Lakeway proper, an upscale community of resort houses with a view of Lake Travis. Instead, Estrada's place, according to Meecham's GPS, was northeast of Lakeway in a sparsely populated area.

An area where dirty deeds could be clandestinely conducted.

As the Mercedes climbed higher in the hilly terrain and the lights of the city had given way to an eerie darkness, his sense of remoteness grew. They had passed only one vehicle. He fleetingly felt sorry for the van's driver who had to rise so early in the morning to make an honest day's wages.

But most of his thoughts centered on Ava. In his mind's eye he kept picturing her lovely body lying in a pool of blood, her throat slashed like Elaine Meecham's. That was when he understood what she had meant in the warehouse when she'd said she wouldn't want to live without him.

For he felt exactly the same.

Such a horrible, horrible shame that it had taken them nine years of aimless loneliness to realize they belonged together. Nine years of happiness they could have shared.

There was no longer room in his heart for anger toward her. All he felt was an intense love. For a brief time the previous night he'd recaptured that consuming love they'd experienced as teenagers. His heart literally ached now at the memory of her bare flesh pressed against his on the sofa at their safe house, of those minutes of sheer bliss he'd known in her arms, bliss he might never know again.

Unless he found her. Quickly.

He vowed to push his manly pride aside and beg her for a reconciliation — if she were still alive.

His stomach churned so sluggishly he felt as if he were carsick. And Blake had never been carsick in his life. He found himself praying that she still be alive.

"I think we should call in the police," Pete said. "We know they've already murdered Mrs. Meecham, and they're threatening a child and Ava."

"No!" Meecham hissed. "If police surround the house, they might kill Mick."

"He's right," Blake said. "Besides, now that I know Estrada's got a man in the PD on his payroll, I know that dirty cop could tip off

Estrada that the police were closing in. We can't risk the boy or Ava."

"Then we'd better have a damn good plan," Pete said.

"There are three of us. And we'll have the element of surprise. Chances are those scumbags are still sleeping right now."

"How many do you think there will be?" Pete asked.

"I would think four, tops." Blake eyed the car's navigation system screen. "We're close. Just four-tenths of a mile away." He turned to Meecham. "Let's pull up into that next dirt driveway and into some brush to hide the vehicle."

"Good idea," Pete agreed. "We'll walk the rest of the way."

As soon as the car was parked and they got out of the vehicle, Blake smelled fire. Could it be from a chimney? Heck, this was May, far too hot for that.

Then, his stomach dropped. Stark terror surged through him. "I smell smoke!" He took off running toward Estrada's house, deep in the woods.

When they reached a clearing, he saw the flames. As instinctively as Ava had known from her dreams that Mick was in danger, he knew Ava was in that burning house. "Ava!" he yelled, sprinting toward the house as if a fire were breathing down his back.

Pete sprinted after him. "What in the hell

are you doing?"

"I'm going in there! Call 9-1-1!" If Ava was in there, and if he could reach her in time, she would almost certainly need medical attention.

He rushed to the back of the house, where the flames brightened the night sky. "Ava!" he cried. *Please let her hear me.* "Ava!"

"Help me, Blake!" It was the most beautiful sound he'd ever heard. From her voice, he pinpointed her location. She was close to the source of the fire, near the window where the fire was most intense.

He wouldn't be able to enter there.

He hurried to the next window, smashed it with the handle of his revolver, and climbed in. Disappointment surged through him when he realized this wasn't the room where she was. "Ava!"

"I'm here. Please hurry."

He darted into the hallway where thick, graphite smoke billowed. He couldn't see a thing. He tried to recall those lessons about surviving a fire. *Smoke rises.* Lowering himself to a dog position, he crawled through the smoke until he reached the next doorway. "Ava!" he called.

No response.

Oh, God, I'm too late.

Even through smoke so thick he would not have been able to see his own hand, he saw the blaze of orange flames encroaching on the whole room like ink on a tissue. The heat was so intense, the hairs on his arm singed. He began to cough, his airways closing.

Fear pulsing through him, he briefly thought, *I can't go there.* But he told himself *I must. If I die, I die beside her.*

Coughing with every breath, he stormed into the thick smoke.

Since he couldn't see anything but flames and a screen of smoke that looked like impenetrable clouds, he had to hope he'd ram into her. She would probably be tied to a chair or bed.

The smoke inhalation must be having a hallucinogenic effect on him. He felt as if he were inhaling sand, and his lungs were slowly filling with it as his breath was being squeezed away like liquid through a dropper.

His head, less than three feet off the ground due to his doggie position, collided with the side of a mattress. Coughing uncontrollably, he felt the top of the mattress. His hand touched flesh. He patted up her leg until he felt rope, then took out his Swiss Army knife and cut through it from the inside out.

There was no time to feel for a pulse. He had to get her out of there. Which meant he'd have to stand in order to lift her. He withdrew a handkerchief and covered his mouth and nose as he stood, but when he reached down to lift her, the white scrap of fabric fell.

His heart beating out of control, he felt the fire's heat, saw that it had spread now to within feet of them. He pulled her into his arms and sprinted like hell for the door.

This time he raced to the front of the house, where the fire had not reached, and flew out the door — blessedly — into fresh air.

An emergency vehicle, its lights flashing and siren screeching, sped up the dirt driveway and slammed to a halt in front of the house. It was a fire truck. Following it, an ambulance.

In less than a minute he was sucking oxygen, and the pair of paramedics were attending Ava.

"You could have been killed!" Pete chastised.

Blake kept watching Ava. "Is she. . .alive?"

"Yeah, they found a pulse."

The knowledge was no consolation. He wouldn't feel relief until he saw her move. And, dammit, she wasn't moving!

Walter Meecham stood silently beside him. "I didn't expect Mick to be there," he finally said. "I had demanded that I hear my boy's voice before I go on that witness stand tomorrow. They'll keep him alive until then."

"Then we've got to find him before then," Blake said, never removing his eyes from Ava. What in the hell had those monsters done to her? Her shoulder wound had bled through the thick bandage, permeating most of her tank top with the dark stain of blood. Even her face — her lovely, lovely face — was streaked with blood. He'd like to kill the sons of bitches who had left her to die.

As he watched, she began to stir. He tossed off the oxygen mask and moved to her, as did Meecham. Her eyes flicked open, and she saw Blake. A smile tilted the corners of her mouth. "You found me."

"Where's my boy?" Meecham demanded of her.

She looked up at him, her face puzzled.

"He's not what you thought, Ava," Blake said. "Estrada abducted Mick as insurance that Meecham recount his eye witness testimony against Pacheco."

"So that's why they kept him alive," she said, her voice weak and scratchy.

"Was he here?" Blake asked.

She nodded.

Meecham pressed closer to her. "Do you know where they've taken him?"

She sat up. "To Del Valle!"

Blake turned to Meecham. "I've got the address. Let's go."

"I'll go get the car," Meecham said.

Blake directed his attention to the paramedics. "She needs to be taken to the hospital."

"No!" she shrieked, rising. Then she closed her eyes, a look of gratitude on her face. "I thought I was paralyzed when Estrada knocked me to the ground, but I can move! And I'm going with you."

"You're sure as hell *not* going with us," Blake countered.

She addressed the paramedics: "You can go now. I'm refusing further treatment."

Blake looked at the men as they shrugged. "Sorry, sir, but we can't force a conscious patient to go to the hospital."

"I promise, Blake, as soon as I see Mick safely delivered from those awful men, I'll return to the hospital." Tears filled her eyes as she spoke to Blake in a low voice. "I met him. I vowed to protect him. Don't you see I have to be there for him?"

He faced the paramedics. "In your opinion, is her condition life threatening?"

"Her blood pressure's high, and she's definitely running fever, but, no, sir, I wouldn't think it's life threatening. At least not at the present."

Shaking his head with disapproval, Blake lifted her and began to carry her to Meecham's awaiting car. He and Ava got in the back, and he continued to hold her against him, treasuring the feel of a living, breathing Ava.

From the front seat, Pete's head swiveled. "So you're Ava. I've heard about you for a long time."

"And you must be Pete," she said, snaking

her arm around Blake's midsection. "It's nice to meet you."

"Are you sure you guys don't want to bring in the police?" Pete asked. "It could take us an hour to get to Del Valle from here."

"Not in my car," Meecham said, "and not at this time of night." He patted his dash.

"But it could be daylight before we get there," Pete protested.

Meecham shook his head. "We'll be there before daybreak."

"Do you know how much of a head start they had?" Blake asked Ava.

She shrugged. "I'd guess ten minutes. That's all."

"Hell, we could overtake them," Pete said.

"What kind of vehicle were they in?" Blake asked Ava.

"A van. I think it was white."

* * *

She had lain in the room, flames devouring the wall not more than ten feet from her and smoke as thick as a velvet curtain making it impossible for her to see even her own feet. *Let me die of asphyxiation* she had prayed. She wished to be spared the agony of burning to death.

On the very brink of death, she heard Blake calling her name. Somehow, he had found her. Joy had filled her soul even as she thought he could die trying to save her. They might die together.

That thought was the last thing she remembered.

Blake — her most precious Blake — had, indeed, risked his life to save hers.

Now, as they sped through the dark she rested her face against the solidness of his chest, felt his arm close around her. She never wanted him to leave her side for as long as she lived. Could he possibly feel the same?

"If you weren't so damned sick, I'd give you a good spanking," he said. "Why in the hell didn't you tell *me* when you started to run fever?"

"You had to keep looking for Mick."

"You almost got yourself killed."

"So did you!" she said. "No one in his right mind would run into a burning house to rescue someone who needed a good spanking."

"I guess where you're concerned, I'm not in my right mind, then."

Was that a declaration? That was probably as close as Blake would come to telling her he might be in love with her.

And that was just fine with her. Actions spoke louder than words.

A deep, satisfying smile on her face, she closed her eyes, drifting into a contented slumber in Blake's embrace.

She woke when the car stopped and she heard the jingle of keys being withdrawn from the ignition. "I think it's that white house with the van in front," Meecham said.

Ava sat up and surveyed their surroundings the best she could, given that it was still dark. Like the house near Lakeway, this one was isolated from any nearby neighbors. It was a typical rural Texas house, a white frame square on a pier-and-beam foundation. The dirt lane that served as a road in front of the house was guttered on either side by narrow drainage ditches.

Since it was closer to metropolitan Austin, the darkness was not as intense as it had been north of Lakeway. They had parked down the street a couple of hundred yards away.

"There's a light on," Pete said.

Blake frowned. "Which means they're all awake."

"And probably alert," Meecham added.

"We'll have to split up and come from three separate directions," Blake said, turning to Ava. "How many are there?"

She shrugged. "Estrada and four young thugs. Mickey's hands and feet were bound, and duct tape covered his mouth. I don't know, though, if any other of the creeps might already have been here in Del Valle."

"I wouldn't think so since there's only the van," Blake said.

"We're seriously outnumbered," Meecham said.

"But Blake and I are marksmen," Pete

added.

Blake frowned again. "Without rifles with scopes."

"I, uh," Pete said, "grabbed my extra pistol from the glove box, Meecham, in case you'd like to be armed."

"I sure as hell do."

"I'm glad you're with us, Meecham," Blake said. "The boy won't be afraid when he sees you. Our priority is to get him out of the house. If we have to take out the bastards, so be it."

"Mr. Meecham's right!" Ava said. "You'll be seriously outnumbered."

Pete faced Ava. "But we do have the element of surprise."

"When you arrived at the lake house," Blake questioned Ava, "was Mick shut up in a room by himself?"

She nodded. "The room was locked, and its window was boarded."

"Let's hope it's the same setup again," Blake said. "We look for a boarded window first. If there is one, that's where Mick will be."

"Then we gotta hope he's alone in that room," Pete said.

Blake nodded. "I'll go through neighboring property which looks to be nothing more than pasture. I'll circle around and approach the house from the back."

"I'll do the same on the other side," Pete

said.

"What will I do?" Meecham asked.

"I want you with me," Blake said, "to reassure Mick."

Meecham agreed.

"And just so that I don't stand out in the night," Blake said, "I'm taking off this damned white shirt. Again." The two other men wore dark clothing. Blake unbuttoned the shirt and shrugged out of it.

Ava studied his perfect body as if she would never see it again.

"You, young lady," Blake said, "are staying in the car."

She nodded. "You have enough to deal with without worrying about me."

He opened the car door and went to get out. "Here take my cell."

She took it, then touched his bare arm. "Be careful."

He nodded and stepped from the vehicle.

"Blake?"

He turned back.

"I love you."

"I love you, too." Then he eased the door shut, drew his gun, and walked into the neighboring pasture, Meecham walking abreast of him and Pete approaching the house from the opposite side.

Ava watched Blake until he and Meecham merged into the darkness.

Five minutes passed. Slow, terror-filled

minutes when a thousand scenarios rushed through her mind.

Then she heard the horrifying sound of a gun discharging.

Chapter 16

Blake and Meecham had cleared the first hurdle by reaching the rear of the house undetected. They went straight for the window that had been boarded over with weathered cedar. There was no need for words. Both of them knew their son was behind that window, probably still bound and gagged.

Blake's first priority was to yank those boards off. He flashed his penlight on it and discovered the window had been secured with a section of discarded fencing that was held together by a single cross board. Only two nails — one at the top of the window frame and the other at the bottom — fastened the fencing to the house's exterior, rotting wood. One quick grip and he'd pulled the fencing from the window.

He aimed his flashlight into the room, and when he saw the boy curled up on the bed, the child's eyes wide with fright, something inside Blake melted. A sense of relief rushed over him when he saw the boy was alone.

He quickly flashed the light onto

Meecham's face to give the child assurance. Then for the second time that night, Blake cut a hole in the glass, unlatched the window lock, and raised the window's lower section. He climbed into the dark room first, then assisted Meecham.

Blake stood guard, his gun aimed at the door, while Meecham hurried to the child and embraced him, whispering something Blake could not hear. Then the boy's adoptive father lifted him into his arms and scurried back to the window.

By then, Pete was standing outside, and Meecham silently handed Mick into his arms before he climbed out, followed by Blake. Pete stood the boy up and slashed through the ropes that bound him, then, index fingers to his lips, he pulled away the duct tape from his mouth.

Blake pointed down the street, in the direction of the Mercedes, and whispered, "Run! Your dad's car is over there. Run to it."

Mick took off like a bullet.

Pete faced Blake, holding up a halting hand as he listened to the voices raised in Spanish coming from the lone, lighted room. "One of them heard something outside," he translated, his voice barely above a whisper. "We'd better get the hell out of here."

All three men took off running. The front door of the house burst open. Still running, Blake turned his head. And saw one of those shaved-headed bastards standing beneath the porch light, a large pistol in his hand, his other hand bracing for a shoot.

His first thought was the man was going to shoot Mick. He stopped and spread his feet wide, taking aim at the guy on the porch.

But he was too late. The man's pistol discharged.

Blake took him out, then braced to face the reinforcements. He knew there were four more men in that house.

Glass shattered. The others were taking positions at the windows.

He wondered if they could see him in such darkness. He wondered if he should stay there and shoot or try to get the hell away from there as fast as he could.

Another gun discharged, but this time the noise came from closer to the street, not from the house. Pete? Had Pete been able to take out one the guys at the windows? He was a hell of a marksman, and he had excellent night vision.

In all likelihood, these wannabe hoods weren't nearly as well trained as he and Pete. He decided to take his chances running away. How good of shots could they be? A moving target — at night — was no easy hit.

Besides, if Mick had been hit, he needed to get him medical help. Quickly.

Halfway between his position and the street, he nearly stumbled over a body.

Meecham's. He dropped to his knees to feel for a pulse. It was very faint. "Can you make it, man?" he asked, sympathy in his voice.

"I don't . . . think so," Meecham gasped. "Take care of my boy. He be. . .belongs with you now." Then his labored breathing ceased.

* * *

Her first instinct when she heard the shot was to run to Blake, but logic overruled instinct. She called 9-1-1 and in a calm voice that belied the shaking fear roiling through her, she gave the female dispatcher the address and told her a shootout was in progress.

"How many involved in the altercation?" the female asked.

"Five criminals and three good guys who were attempting to rescue a kidnapped child."

"We'll have someone there as soon as possible."

As soon as the call was disconnected, she heard the pounding of feet racing toward the car and looked up to see Mick, his legs moving like greased wheels.

She leapt from the car and rushed to embrace him, cherishing the feel of his sturdy little body in her arms. *He's safe.*

"You kept your promise to me," he said in that husky yet youthful voice which now shook on every vowel.

"I did. I did. But I had lots of help from people who love you." She kept an arm around him and walked him to the car. "I need you to get in the car, lock the doors, and lie on the floor."

"But what about you? What about my daddy?"

"Don't worry about us, my darling. Just do as I say. Please."

In the distance she heard the sirens.

* * *

Blake had taken down one of Estrada's hired guns, Pete took the one at the window. Both were dead. Once the police surrounded the house with megaphones, sharpshooters, and finally, tear gas, the other three were coaxed from the house, arms high above their heads.

As much as Blake did not want to do it, he knew the boy had to be told about his father. He explained that Walter Meecham was a hero whose family had been jeopardized because he was doing the right thing and standing up against evil. He was a noble man who had died to protect his son.

"And my mother? She's dead, too, isn't she?" Mick had asked.

"Yes, my darling," Ava answered. "I'm so sorry."

He cried as only a child can cry, with deep, shaking sobs. Blake took him in his arms and, with Ava at their side, took him to the paramedics. He needed something to calm him, to provide the sleep denied him the previous night.

Both Mick and Ava were transported to the hospital, where Blake met them. While Ava was given an I.V. of antibiotics, Mick — on a gurney beside her — was given a sedative. It calmed his hysterics almost immediately, and as he was groggily drifting off into sleep he asked, "Will I have to live in an orphanage?"

"Certainly not," Ava said.

"My parents weren't my real parents," he slurred. "I'm adopted. Maybe I could find my real parents, and they would want me now."

Tears came to Ava's eyes. "Honey, your real parents have only ever wanted what's best for you. They love you very much."

A half smile on his drowsy face, he looked from one to the other. "I think you're my real parents."

Blake's eyes moist, his voice hoarse with emotion, he stepped up to his son, placed his hand on the boy's shoulder, and said, "I think you're right, son."

* * *

Once Ava finished her treatment and saw a physician who redressed the wound and told her to curtail all activity, Blake took her and the sleeping child to their safe house, where the police met them to get a full statement.

After more than two hours, the police had the complete story, including the information that one of their own officers was on the take.

The detective who came to them explained that Estrada had been one of the fatalities, and that one of the gang members who had been taken into custody was already cutting a deal to testify against Pacheco in exchange for leniency in his own charges.

As soon as the police left, without saying anything to one another, Blake and Ava went straight to the door of the bedroom where their child slept so peacefully. Their hands clasped together, they stood there watching him for several minutes, drinking in the wonder of him.

Finally Blake insisted that she lie down, and he came to sit on the bed beside her. "The doctor said no activity," she said playfully, "so don't be getting any ideas."

"I do have an idea. I need you to help me keep a promise I made to a dying man."

Her face went serious. "To Walter Meecham?"

He nodded.

"Yes?"

"He wanted me to take care of Mick."

Her heart fluttered. She thought she knew what was coming next. "Yes?"

"I'm going to need help. I was thinking maybe we could, uh, you know, get married and all, make a home for the kid."

She smirked. "You'd be willing to make such a sacrifice for Mick?"

He turned serious, his voice softening.

"Come on, Ava, you know I'm crazy about you. Always have been."

She launched herself into his arms. "Oh, Blake, I've made mistakes, but I'm not going to botch it this time like I did nine years ago. You're the only man I could ever spend my life with, the only man I'll ever love."

He tenderly eased her back to the mattress. "Remember, no activity."

And then he kissed her thoroughly.

Epilogue

One year later

Mick sat between Ava and Blake in the pickup as they cruised through the late-afternoon traffic.

"I think today was my happiest day ever," the child said.

Ava smiled at the boy who so thoroughly owned her heart. "I hope you're not just saying that because you got out of school."

He shook his head. "Well, that part was pretty cool, too. That judge was really nice."

She had thought so, too, when Judge Lampkin said Mick's was the most heart-warming adoption case she had ever presided over and when she had smiled down at Mick and told him he was a very fortunate little boy to have been loved so much by two sets of parents. "Yes, she was nice."

"I liked the part when you told her you and . . . my Dad were the luckiest couple in the world."

"We meant every word, son." Blake did not remove his eyes from his driving as he slanted his truck into a parking space.

"Dad?" Mick looked up at Blake when he turned off the ignition. "I've been thinking about what the judge told me about it being my choice if I wanted to keep the Meecham name or take yours."

Blake stilled, not making eye contact with his son. "And?"

"And I think I'd like to keep Meecham as my middle name, but I'm ready to be known as Coach Tranowski's son." His whipped around to Ava. "And yours, too, Mom."

Mom. The most precious name she'd ever been called. "It's always been your choice, my sweetie." She hugged him before he got out of the car. "You've made us pretty darn happy." Her glance flicked to Blake as he opened the door and stepped down. His eyes had moistened.

"How about helping your old man carry some of this equipment?"

"Sure thing, Coach," Mick said.

She kept her distance behind her two fellows as they walked side by side, baseball gear hoisted over their shoulders, the Little League field where bleachers were beginning to fill, their destination. It was uncanny how similar father and son were, right down to the gait in their walk.

Some of her happiest hours had been spent here at this very ball park. But then, ever since those cries in the night restored her baby – and Blake – to her, Ava had been deliriously happy.

After tossing the catcher his gear, Blake glanced up to her, seated in her usual second-row seat, and almost without being aware of what he was doing because it came so naturally to him, he threw her a kiss.

Now her eyes filled with tears. This wasn't just Mick's happiest day ever. It was hers, too.

The End

Texas Heroines in Peril

If you enjoyed reading *A Cry In The Night,* you may also enjoy the other three installments of *Texas Heroines in Peril:*

Protecting Britannia
(Texas Heroines in Peril Series)

"Drawing on her real-life expertise as a dealer in British antiques, Cheryl Bolen pens a fast-paced, fascinating tale of modern-day romantic suspense." – *Colleen Thompson, Rita finalist romantic suspense*

"It's fun to watch the case unfold in this nonstop action adventure. 4 Stars" – *Romantic Times magazine*

* * *

Antiques dealer Britannia Hensley's first day back in London after a seven-year absence seems like an audition for a Survivor in the City episode. Her plane arrives two hours late; she sloshes through blinding rain without an umbrella; her purse is snatched; her hotel room ransacked; some slimeball jabs a gun into her back and tries to abduct her; and every bobby in London's after her for a murder she didn't commit. What's a girl to do when she has no passport, no money, no means of getting any money, and no one she can call? Well, actually there is someone . . . but surely after all these years a handsome guy like Graham's been snatched up by some lucky girl.

Murder at Veranda House
(Texas Heroines in Peril Series)

Lovely young widow Annette Holcombe is forced to turn her Veranda House on Galveston Island into a B & B after the recent death of her husband, a man she'd known only a short time. Upon his untimely death, she learns that the only thing she really knew about him was that everything she knew about him was a lie!

And if being penniless wasn't bad enough, now Annette's got to contend with threatening letters, suspicious guests, fears for her daughter's safety, an impending hurricane—and murder! If only there was someone to trust. Someone like Dr. Grant Garrison, a personable, good-looking guest who's teaching at the island's medical school.

But Grant, too, isn't what he seems.

Capitol Offense
(Texas Heroines in Peril Series)

As speech writer to the Texas lieutenant governor, lovely Lacy Blair accidentally stumbles onto a high-level fraud involving state funds and masterminded by her boss. Since she can't risk snooping into the situation herself, she secretly consults with an FBI agent who agrees to help her investigate. Soon afterwards, she realizes she is being watched, and the FBI agent has been killed.

Terrified for her own safety and hungry for justice, she flees. But where can she turn? Who can she trust? Her former lover, Mike Talamino, is the only person she could ever count on. But will he agree to help her? Can she endanger him, too?

Author's Biography

A former journalist who, in her own words, has "a fascination with dead Englishwomen," Cheryl Bolen is the award-winning author of more than a dozen historical romance novels set in Regency England, including *Marriage of Inconvenience*, *My Lord Wicked*, and *A Duke Deceived*. Her books have received numerous awards, such as the 2011 International Digital Award for Best Historical Novel and the 2006 Holt Medallion for Best Historical. She was also a 2006 finalist in the Daphne du Maurier for Best Historical Mystery. Her works have been translated into eleven languages and have been Amazon.com bestsellers. Bolen has contributed to *Writers Digest* and *Romance Writers Report* as well as to the Regency era–themed newsletters *The Regency Plume, The Regency Reader*, and *The Quizzing Glass*. The mother of two grown sons, she lives with her professor husband in Texas.

Made in the USA
Las Vegas, NV
25 April 2024

89130584R00132